THE ZONE

#6

PLAGUE BOMB

Books by James Rouch

The Zone Series
#1: Hard Target
#2: Blind Fire
#3: Hunter Killer
#4: Sky Strike
#5: Overkill
#6: Plague Bomb
#7: Killing Ground
#8: Civilian Slaughter
#9: Body Count
#10: Death March

World War II Collection
#1: The War Machines
#2: Tiger
#3: Gateway to Hell

THE ZONE

#6

PLAGUE BOMB

James Rouch

SPEAKING VOLUMES, LLC
NAPLES, FLORIDA
2013

THE ZONE
PLAGUE BOMB #6

ISBN 978-1-61232-913-0

INTELLIGENCE EVALUATION. CIA FOR PRESIDENT. COPIES
. . . SECRETARY OF STATE FOR DEFENSE . . . JOINT
CHIEFS OF NATO STAFF . . . MI6

AFTER SEVERAL RECENT SOVIET PROPAGANDA RE-
VERSES IT IS LIKELY THE KGB WILL BE SEEKING MEANS
BY WHICH TO EMBARRASS THE NATO POWERS AND
SHOW THE USSR AND THE WARSAW PACT IN A GOOD
LIGHT THROUGH FAVORABLE WORLD WIDE PUBLICITY IN
THE WEEKS BEFORE THE CRUCIAL CONFERENCE OF
NEUTRAL NATIONS.

WHILE IT MUST BE THOUGHT UNLIKELY THAT THE
KGB WILL TOTALLY FABRICATE AN INCIDENT, ESPE-
CIALLY AFTER THE EXPOSURE AND FAILURE OF THEIR
ATTEMPT TO SUBVERT THE NORWEGIAN PARLIAMENT'S
VOTE ON NEUTRALITY, IT IS PROBABLE THAT THEY WILL
USE "SLEEPERS" AND "AGENTS OF INFLUENCE" TO INITI-
ATE SOME DRAMATIC ACT, POSSIBLY BY A WESTERN
PACIFIST OR DISARMAMENT GROUP.

IT IS LIKELY THAT DEPARTMENT A OF THE KGB'S
FIRST CHIEF DIRECTORATE WILL BE RESPONSIBLE FOR
ANY SUCH OPERATION, SO MAKING THE CHOICE OF THE
NEW HEAD OF THAT DEPARTMENT OF ACUTE INTEREST
TO WESTERN INTELLIGENCE AGENCIES.

A PROFILE AND EVALUATION OF THE OFFICER AP-
POINTED WILL BE CIRCULATED AS SOON AS HIS IDENTIFI-
CATION HAS BEEN CONFIRMED.

CHAPTER ONE

There were less than a hundred names on the death warrant. It would be an easy day for the Lubyanka's execution squad.

Col. Yuri Rozenkov took up his pen, and not bothering to first remove the accumulated fluff from its nib, started to scrawl and gouge his signature, then stopped. It would be a good opportunity to try his new toy. From a drawer he took the ink pad and the as yet unstained stamp. He crushed its mirror image carved head into the oozing dark blue cushion, then pounded it onto the coarse grained paper at the foot of the list of names.

That was another eighty-nine files that could be closed, but by the end of the day at least that number of new ones would be opened, as the prison took in its quota. Most likely there would be more walking in than carried out, and the problems of severe over-crowding would become that much worse.

Without even glancing at the double column of single spaced names, Rozenkov moved the sheet to his out-tray. His eyes strayed to the telephone as he groped, without looking, for the next list. It did not ring, and he forced his attention back to the paper-work.

On this the close-typed names were broken into sections of roughly equal length by sub-headings. These were the prisoners who retained some vestige of their former health and sanity after the KGB's expert interrogators had finished their work. Among them would be a few who had never even been to the underground rooms where that was done. Some were unfortunates who had been sent by mistake, who had been intended for less rigorous establishments, others had arrived in demented state, driven insane by fear of what they knew lay ahead even before they had crossed the threshold. There was not the time to sort and redirect them.

Those on the list were unique among the prison's inmates, they were among the tiny minority who left it alive, but they were unlikely to survive long. The chemical and medical experimental establishments had seemingly insatiable demands for human guinea pigs. Some were going to the Institute for Blood Research here in Moscow, on Moznayskoye road, others to the biological weapons research establishment at Sverdlovsk.

Again he looked at the telephone, still sentient on the edge of his desk. Had he over-played his hand? He knew his ambition was recognized and had worked hard to give it the image of a virtue. A promotion was due to him and with the arrest of General Khramoveski a path had opened that could, that must, lead to a plum position.

The colonel tensed and half reached for it as the instrument gave a brief half-hearted jingle and no more. Forgetting the new stamp he slashed his signature across the paper and slapped it on top of the others. A knock on the door was hesitant, light, almost feeble.

"Enter."

A senior sergeant took a half pace into the room, holding a strip of teleprinter readout before him like a talisman. "From the Department of Administration, Comrade Colonel."

"Well?" Rozenkov knew the effect his sharp tone would have on the NCO. He had cultivated its menace during the years he had worked with the interrogation units. There were times when it had been successful where acid and electric shock treatment and even drugs had failed. It worked now, and the sergeant's hand shook visibly.

"They . . . the Department of . . . they wish to know if we can take another three hundred prisoners today. There has been a riot at Psychiatric Hospital number seven, on Institutskii Lane . . ."

"Impossible, tell them . . ." Rozenkov paused. Of course it was impossible, physically impossible to cram any more bodies into the prison, many were dying of disease before they could be questioned, and the guards themselves were beginning to succumb to the building's foul atmosphere. The stench was even starting to permeate to this office. They must be fools in administration, they knew the position . . . They knew! Of course they knew; he was being tested.

"Tell them we will be ready in one hour. Make the reply immediately, then contact the chief officer and senior warder from each floor. I want them here in thirty, no, ten minutes. Each of them to have a list of fifty names. Contact all our experimental establishments, tell them we can supply all their needs, all of them. Then alert the commander of the execution squad, tell him to have his men draw extra ammunition and stand by. Arrange transport for upwards of two hundred bodies. Well, get to it man, now!"

The sergeant disappeared, and the closing of the door wafted the stink of human waste about the room. Rozenkov didn't notice it, and wouldn't as it became stronger, as it would, as it always did when a clear-out was initiated. Fear would spread through the Lubyanka like a raging contagion and sheer terror would in some cases do the executioners' work for them. When the killing began, and much of it would be done in the cells where all could hear, there would be a number of prisoners whose hearts would give out, who would die of fear. It might be as many as four or five of the inmates. Another eight or more would self-inflict fatal injuries on themselves, despite the constant searches geared to deprive them of any weapon that might serve that or any other lethal purpose.

And at least one guard, possibly two, would be killed or maimed by the frenzied resistance as tiring in their work, they became careless, let drop their concentration for even a moment.

Colonel Rozenkov did not care. He had set the slaughter in motion and with only deft guiding touches it would roll through the building until the floors ran with blood and the killers became too exhausted to kill.

It was several years since he'd actually participated in such an event, not since he'd led the first assault platoon in the retaking of the huge Prasnya transit prison in Moscow's Kradnaya district. That had been a blood bath. Some of his heavily armed shock troops had been literally torn apart by the rioting inmates, had gone down under an avalanche of fists and feet to be ripped open by nails and teeth.

That day he had killed twenty or more of the prisoners himself, perhaps twice that number, he'd not kept a count. He could recall standing off from a group cowering in a corner of a dimly lit cell and emptying his pistol into them, then closing with a bayonet fitted AK74 to whittle the huddling would-be escapers down to more manageable numbers, using his skills at inflicting painful death to peel away the outer layers of the hysterical press until with his bare hands he had throttled its last surviving member.

He fingered the slight ridge of a circular scar on the back of his hand where a shattered stub of a light bulb had momentarily been used as an effective weapon against him.

Insulated as he was by half the width of the huge building from the Lubyanka's cell block, Rozenkov couldn't hear the clamor that would be starting, but he knew it would have. It didn't matter, the thought like the sound was blocked from his mind. He had eyes and ears only for the telephone.

The horror that was the Soviet Union's most notorious prison no longer concerned him. It had never been more than a stepping stone on the way to greater things, to higher rank and position. In his time there he had signed away lives beyond number, hardly knowing, not caring whose they were . . . but it was in a way fitting that his departure should be marked

11

by this last slaughter . . . And he had thought that the execution squads were in for an easy day . . .

It took an effort of will, but he let the telephone ring twice before snatching it from its cradle.

The Rangerover's two-tone blue over gray paintwork had been heavily smeared with mud, and sprays and bundles of wilting foliage festooned it haphazardly, inexpertly secured to any projection and wedged into every joint between the panels.

Four civilian passengers sat inside, a fifth stood beside the vehicle using powerful binoculars to scan the road ahead. Several times the observer panned the winding route, until a distant scene of activity caught his attention and was brought into focus. He stood for a moment, concentrating his attention, then lowered his glasses and flicked through an artwork illustrated book laid open on the driver's seat.

"We'll have to make another detour." Stopping at a page that showed front and side views of an armored recovery vehicle, he took another look through the glasses to confirm the identification. "There are troops up ahead. Another mile or so and we'd have run straight into them."

"Are they ours?"

A rear window was wound down and Professor Edwards' wrinkled face blinked sharp-eyed inquiry.

"Depends what you mean by ours. Seems to be a NATO group."

The thin-lipped mouth among the wrinkles gave a disparaging grunt and Edwards restored the glass barrier between himself and the world.

Stowing the binoculars in an imitation leather case every bit as scratched and battered as the instrument itself, the observer climbed back into the driving seat, pushing the book in among the crumpled maps filling the parcel shelf. "If you're all ready?"

"I haven't finished my coffee."

Father Venable's reedy voice piped from the far side of the rear seat.

"Well bloody hurry then, we're here to stop a fucking war, not have a sodding picnic." The burly figure whose broad frame dominated the center of the rear seat, without regard for the discomfort he inflicted on the elderly men squeezed on either side of him, glowered at the bespectacled priest. "Be better if you didn't have a drink. Who was it who ever persuaded me to come on this trip with a bus load of incontinent geriatrics?"

"Really . . . there is no need for . . . language . . ."

The driver interjected to cut through the plaintive chorus of protest from the pair being crushed by the big man's contortions as he strove to make himself comfortable. "It'd be a help, Gross, if you cut out the personal abuse, saved it for your shop stewards' meetings, and if the rest of you rose less swiftly to his bait."

"Sir Julian is quite right." Nodding agreement with their driver, Professor Edwards gave up the unequal struggle to try to obtain a more equitable share of the available space and sought distraction in a contribution to the discussion. "We should recall our mission, its purpose. For the sake of that, for appearance's sake, we should strive to achieve a degree of harmony. I must myself admit, that while I cannot subscribe to

13

so optimistic a projection of the outcome of our endeavors we must not let petty differences blind us to the importance . . ."

"Aw, shut it, you prissy asshole." The CND badge pinned to the left breast of the stained fawn anorak worn by the woman in the front passenger seat rose and fell significantly as she let out a long sigh. She leaned across and spoke to their driver as he steered them on to a fresh heading that would take them past the NATO troops. "Jesus Webb, did you say that Edwards had won a Nobel prize? What for, hot air and bullshit?"

Webb glanced at the woman, able to spare only that moment as the potholed surface and the many broken boughs that littered it tested even the Rover's rugged suspension and power steering. "He was espousing the cause of disarmament before you were born, let alone before you decided you weren't much good as an actress and there might be more in it for you to make yourself into a pale imitation of Jane Fonda."

"He got you there." Gross leaned forward and turned a wet-lipped rubbery leer to the women. "Be warned little starlet, little aging starlet, Sir Julian here has crossed verbal swords with better men and women than you. For years he's been virtually a compulsory member of every expert panel on television and radio in England. He's made more in appearance fees than you have hooking on Broadway between walk-on parts, or should I say lie-down parts."

"That'll do Gross, let it go at that." Wrenching the wheel hard over, Webb didn't quite succeed in avoid-

14

ing a deep hole where a drain cover had collapsed.

From Father Venables came a yelp as the vehicle lurched. A garishly colored flask jumped from his hand, bounced against the fabric lining of the roof and spattered all the passengers with lukewarm coffee.

Again Webb caught a glimpse of the woman, this time as she tried to cover her head against the sticky deluge. She wasn't completely successful and the sweet fluid trickled through her plastered hair and down her cheek. Immediately she set to work to repair the damage, using tissues and cosmetics from a small bag pulled from the depths of a pocket. He wondered how much effort went into cultivating her outdoor look.

The grubby jacket hugging close to her curves, the tight faded jeans; it was all carefully contrived, like her carelessly attractive hair style. But as she worked fast with comb and make-up for an instant he saw the real Sherry Kane, frightened of being a shade over thirty, trying hard to stay in the mold, maintain the image she liked to see of herself. As repairs to hair and face were completed, her style returned and she launched back into character.

"Can we get around that position, or are we likely to be up to our fannies in NATO boy scouts any minute?"

That conjured an absurd and amusing picture, and Webb was surprised that Gross didn't jump in with something suitably suggestive and crude. Possibly the picture wasn't so outlandish; perhaps not boy scouts, but Webb could imagine her going with younger men, much younger . . . "It's not a position. We're far out in front of any fixed defensive lines, have been for the last six hours. Actually there are other parts of the Zone we could have driven across in that time, if there hadn't been the certainty of our being spotted within a few miles. Here it's going to take us a day or so, but the ground forces are far more thinly spread and there's a good chance we'll be able to slip between them. Besides, the more arduous the journey the greater the gesture, and its publicity value."

"What were those troops then?" Venables resecured the top of the all but empty flask.

"Pioneers, I should think, a pick and shovel company cleaning up after the fighting, poor devils, too stupid even to be used as cannon fodder. Not the sort we have to worry about. We can forget them; they'll not be bothering us."

CHAPTER TWO

The Leopard armored recovery vehicle followed Sergeant Hyde and his squad as they walked along the scorched section of road, assessing the suitability of the knocked-out trucks and personnel carriers for repair.

At irregular intervals the surface was pockmarked by shallow indentations where the engineers had removed mines the Russians had found time to plant after springing their ambush on the column.

In many cases there was little of the vehicles left to examine. Fierce blazes had completed the work started by close-range tank fire. Ammunition and fuel loads had burned long enough to totally consume all but steel bodywork and chassis members.

An M113 armored personnel carrier had come to rest a little off the road, having taken only a single hit, and not burned; it looked a more promising candidate for their attention.

The shell's impact had jammed the rear door, and Dooley had to take a crowbar to it. When finally he managed to pry it open the air was suddenly full of fat black flies as a miniature tidal wave of decomposed mushed flesh and bloated maggots slopped slowly around the sides of the partially lowered ramp, and to the ground.

Ripper started to heave, threatened to set others off, until Hyde shoved him away.

Holding a cologne-doused cloth over his mouth and nose, Dooley waved sapper Thorne forward. His voice came indistinctly from behind the rag. "What you waiting for, give it a fucking burst."

"Anything to oblige." As he stepped up, for once he could envy their sergeant. The furnace heat that had long ago destroyed the NCO's face had also ruined his sense of smell. Bracing himself in anticipation of the weapon's surging recoil, Thorne aligned the fuel dribbling nozzle of the man-pack flame thrower on the partially open rear of the carrier.

It bucked in his hands as a three second burst squirted a mushrooming jet of yellow fire, filling his ears with its distinctive wailing screech and washing away the stench of rotting tissue and replacing it with the familiar pungent fumes of unconsumed petrol-jelly.

"Salvage detail, who'd bloody have it. Must be the worst sodding work there is in the whole of the ruddy Zone." A single small arms round cooked off inside, and Burke ducked, expecting more, but there was only the one. "Well isn't it?"

"You don't hear any of us arguing, do you?" Cautiously Dooley approached the combined ramp and door and put his boot onto its warm metal. Using all his weight he tried to force it down further, but it moved only a fraction before its damaged hydraulics locked and prevented any more movement.

Smoke came from scraps of cloth smoldering among the remains inside. Soot stained the metal walls of the interior and coated much of the surface of the sluggish mess oozing toward them.

A neat circular hole marked where the Russian tank shell had penetrated, the APC's bulging and distorted aluminum armor indicated that its explosive filling had detonated inside the crew compartment.

Of the driver and commander and their eleven infantry passengers all that remained was the gelatinous layer of pulped flesh on the floor and bench tops. Fragments of larger bones made it lumpy, as did broken rifles and submachine guns, and crushed helmets holding the pulverized remains of skulls.

A tidy row of boots along either side added a touch of gruesome absurdity. From some protruded the stumps of ankles and from a pair at the far end, untouched by the roaring flame, came a nonstop cascade of squirming white maggots as they overflowed from the heaving food gorged mass that filled them.

"I thought the hygiene squads were supposed to take care of this sort of thing." Not making the mistake of coming too close again, still Ripper had to fight to suppress the urge to retch.

Thorne slipped from the harness of the flame thrower and lowered its triple cylinder pack to the ground, laying it carefully before leaning the hose-linked projector and trigger group against it. A gentle hiss of escaping propellant nitrogen gas came from a pressure tank until he gave its valve an extra half turn. "You're joking. Half the battle damaged armor being back loaded for repair at base workshops has bodies or bits on board. The poor devils from REME who do that job can't cope with it all. Anyway, does the rear-area warriors good to see how mucky the war can be. I'm surprised you're not hardened to it by now. Must be those weird hand-rolled fags you smoke, upsetting your stomach."

"Oh, yeah, and what makes you an authority on everything. Seems to me you ain't so clever, you only just got out after doing twenty-eight days and losing your stripes for impersonating an officer." There was more Ripper would have added, but in his anger at the sapper for mentioning his joints within hearing of the major, he took a step forward too far, and the smell hit him again. He was forced to retreat with his hand clamped tight over his mouth.

"I wouldn't have if your precious major had kept his word and dropped the charges after I knocked out that commie anti-tank position.*

"He's your major as well, now." Sergeant Hyde picked up the flame thrower and thrust it back at the sapper. "You remember that. He'd have willed his soul to the devil, and ours as well, in exchange for the destruction of those Ruskie guns; just be grateful that he spoke up for you at the court martial. You could have gone down for a lot, lot longer."

"Like forever." Setting his head on one side, Dooley let his coated tongue loll from his mouth and made a pantomime of tugging a noose tight about his neck.

"You're not expecting us to shovel this mess, are you." The sentence was phrased precisely by Clarence. It was not a question, it was a statement, a

*Zone 5: Overkill

refusal in advance of any order.

"Heaven forbid that our aseptic sniper should ever be compelled to do such a nasty thing." Using the butt of his rifle, Hyde pushed the door shut as far as it would go. I heard you turned down a medal because you were scared you might have to shake hands with a general at the presentation. If you can't even stand contact with the living then who am I to force you to consort with the dead. Anyway, it's not worth bothering with, it's a write-off."

Those words came as a relief to their Russian deserter. Since Major Revell had gone off to head-quarters to try and get their assignment altered, Boris had been given all of the worst duties by their NCO. In anticipation of being told to climb into the carrier he had already begun to assemble his entrenching tool, now he quietly, and hopefully unobtrusively, stowed it once more. His actions did not entirely escape the sergeant's notice.

"Go tell the ARV crew they can stand down, there's nothing for us here. We'll have a brew then get on to the next site. You know where the tea things are."

All of them stopped, turned and looked as they heard the personnel carrier's door being lowered again. It was Andrea who was surveying the ghastly interior. Her sharp dark eyes met Hyde's.

"Was it like this when your face was destroyed?" Her expression didn't alter as she glanced from the horrors of the vehicle to the sergeant's mask-like graft-built features.

Hyde knew there were few men who could have looked at either without registering at least revulsion.

"No, it was the plasma jet from a hollow-charge warhead that took my face. This looks like it was done by an armor-piercing high explosive round. From the size of the entry hole I'd say about a hundred and twenty-five millimeter. That would make it from a T72 or T84, or maybe an upgunned T64. That what you wanted to know?"

She didn't answer, but walked away, to sit by Boris as he set about boiling water on a small field stove he had scrounged the use of from the young conscript crew of the West German recovery vehicle. Squatting on a wheel blasted from a nearby Mercedes six-wheeler she cradled her grenade discharger fitted M16, her finger hooked casually around the trigger.

Her proximity obviously made the Russian nervous. It took him several attempts before he succeeded in getting the unfamiliar equipment to function correctly, and twice his fumblings almost upset the water.

Hyde had seen her have that effect on others; but then she had some effect on everyone she came in contact with. Among men it varied from manifestations of lust to abject fear, and sometimes both within the space of seconds.

With women the ban of emotive reaction was not as broad, but was within it, if anything, even more pronounced. It was at moments like this, as Hyde caught a good view of her beautiful profile, as even the bulky equipment festooned combat outfit failed to entirely conceal her superb figure, that he could understand their officer's obsession with her. Not that she had ever done anything to encourage the major, the reverse in fact, but the American had fallen in a big way. There were times when it was beginning to have a detrimental effect on the unit's efficiency.

"I been thinking . . ."

"Thought I could smell burning."

Ignoring the sapper's interruption, Dooley went on, ". . . you know I reckon we could have a worse job than this." He grinned and waited for the inevitable response from the expected direction, and wasn't disappointed.

Conscious of being older than the others, Burke had begun to see himself as a father figure. With the pronouncements he made on any and every subject being for the most part ignored by his companions, he'd come to see their silence as unquestioning acceptance of his wisdom, and expected such as his due. Dooley's disagreement with his assessment of their task's lowly status was not well received and he set about unintentionally providing yet more ammunition for the big man's lumbering wit.

"Tell me then, go on, tell me. Here we are, stuck miles forward of our own lines, in an area where we know there's a commie armored battle group operating," sweeping his arms wide he indicated the ambushed and shattered resupply column, "where we could get clobbered ourselves at any moment, and have nothing bigger than a bloody grenade to hit back with, here we are hauling wrecks and shovelling shit. You think you can come up with something worse?"

"Course I can. For a start, we could be ten miles east of here."

"So what's so kinda special about that chunk of the

Zone. Seems to me that one piece of this godforsaken land is pretty much the same as any other." Under cover of the squad's interest in the baiting of their driver, Ripper had rolled and lit a joint. Taking a series of quick draws before extinguishing it and adding it to his meager stock, he saw their sergeant watching him, and almost dropped the tin as he replaced it in his pocket.

"That's where the contamination starts." Clarence knew, like he knew everything there was to know about the Zone. "A year back the communists had a lot of trouble with refugees in that area, too many of them for a start, so word was sent out that they were to be dealt with, reduced to manageable numbers. The local commander must have been short of men and ammunition for his artillery, but he did have two dumps he hadn't used until them, so he emptied them, threw the whole lot into the camps and at any civies who got in the way. We know that one of the dumps held chemical weapons, nerve gas shells, defoliants, toxins, you name it . . ."

"And the other?"

"No one has any idea, at least no one in the west. Must have been batches of experimental weapons. Inside of a week just about every disease you can name, and a lot that haven't even got names yet, was killing the civilians in the hundreds of thousands. All we could do was cordon the sector, treat the few who made it to our side."

"I never read anything about it in the press back home, you sure you got your facts right? Since I've been with your crowd, I've heard some awful tall tales."

"And spun a few yourself." Hyde tapped the medical kit making a prominent bulge in a readily accessible pocket in his jacket. "It's true enough, we were issued with these just after it started. Why it never made the papers God only knows. Probably because we're not so slick at manipulating the world's press, or perhaps some boot licking toady in the British foreign office thought it might upset the Russians, make the negotiated peace that much harder."

"The only thing that happened far as I can see," Burke thought it time he restored some of his authority, "is that we got turned into ruddy pincushions by all those booster shots we started having. Not that I've got any faith in the damned things working, it must be like a bloody germ soup in there. You won't catch me going near the place. If the medics want those injections given field trials they can send some other mug, I won't even go and have a peep over the perimeter wire."

"It ain't right, leaving good land to rot; why don't somebody have a go at it with napalm, or phosphorus, clean it up."

With Burke retreating to a quiet spot to drink his tea, Dooley was happy to shift his attention to Ripper. "Because it'd take forever. We're not talking about a chunk of land the size of a football field, it'd be like trying to sterilize a couple of decent sized counties."

A thousand feet overhead a pilotless sky-spy droned for a while in large circles, chased by lines of flashing orange tracer from the ARVs anti-aircraft machinegun. None of Hyde's squad made any move to copy the aggression and, unharmed, the remotely controlled miniature aircraft went on its way.

"Waste of ammo." With casual interest Hyde tracked the Russian craft, noticing how rarely the tracer came within even a hundred feet of the small camera equipped plane. "On a live firing range back home I watched a whole battalion of armor take turns to have a go at one of those things. For an hour, on and off, it whizzed about sounding like an amplified dentist's drill. They all missed it."

"If the major doesn't get us off this crappy job, and soon, I'll be popping off at the fucking things myself, just to relieve the boredom. Come to that, I'll have a go at anything that beats the monotony of trotting about this truck graveyard." Pulling a face as he tasted his drink and realized it was coffee, Dooley slung it away. "Are we out of the decent stuff again? You know I can't stand this old ladies brew."

"Heck, now I just can't figure that at all." Taking the precaution of stepping beyond Dooley's reach, Ripper displayed his pale green teeth in an ingratiating smile. "From what I hear it kinda seems as how you find the old ladies themselves pretty tasty."

Also expecting retaliation, but far enough away to not to have to take avoiding action himself, Burke waited and watched for it to happen, then swore loud and long as a battle-scarred armored vehicle came clattering down the road toward them, to provide a distraction and diversion. "Bloody hell, I thought I'd seen everything this war had to offer."

The last to do so, even Clarence got to his feet to witness the approach of the Marder personnel carrier. "What on earth is keeping that ancient wreck moving? It looks as if it's spent the last five years as a target on the ranges."

Many of the vehicle's rubber track pads had been worn to pitted wafer-thin shreds, many had gone altogether, and the racket made by the bare metal thrashing the road surface and squealing over the distorted and unlubricated return rollers almost matched that from its rusty and holed exhaust.

Hardly a vestige of paint was to be seen on the gouged and patched armor of its hull and turret. The West German APC bore no unit insignia, nor any other identifying mark, save a partially obliterated white-outlined black Bundeswehr cross on its front.

Slewing to a rocking halt, its clattering diesel raced on after the vehicle had stopped until it at last reluctantly spluttered into clicking silence after a series of gradually diminishing over-runs.

"It will be interesting to see what kind of men would go to war in such a machine." Running his hand over a rough finished irregular patch that only partially concealed a deep hole in the sharply raked upper body, Boris cut his fingers on embedded fragments of tungsten, splinters from the armor-piercing round that had so narrowly failed to penetrate. Fresh blood speckled the metal as he pulled away, and he did so barely in time. The driver's hatch flew open to crash down where his hand had been.

"Then get a mirror, take a good look at yourself." Major Revell pulled himself up until he sat on the hull with his legs dangling into the driving compartment. "Get your gear together, we're moving out."

"In this?" Burke had completed a slow circumnavigation of the Marder, and the curled lip with which he silently signalled his contempt for the transport

27

had grown more pronounced with each step taken and every component investigated.

"That's right, in this. Sorry I couldn't get one with white-walls and a custom paint finish."

"You know me better than that, Major. I don't give a bugger what my wagons look like. They can be papered with candy stripes or stripped to bare metal, doesn't make any difference to me. It's the mechanics I bother about. What I'd like to know is did this crate come to a stop like it did because that's the way you drive, or because its suspension brakes and running gear are knackered?"

"Seen the tracks? The rest of this clunker just about matches them." He was talking to Burke, but Revell was looking at Andrea.

"How long can I have to work on it?" In the APC's condition Burke saw a chance to keep himself out of the firing line for a day or two longer. It'd mean getting dirty, but what with waiting for spares and spinning out the work maybe he could even spin it out to three, or even four, days. So he'd get his hands grubby; better than being shot at.

"You can't. It'll have to do as it is." Revell tried, but he couldn't catch Andrea's eye. She had to be avoiding him deliberately. He heard but didn't pay any heed to their driver's litany of complaint, until he went on too long. "There's a choice. Either we use this heap or we walk. Okay, so if you see it my way, help the others load."

"What have you got us, Major?" Giving up an attempt to wedge a pick and shovel into blast-distorted brackets on the hull side, Sergeant Hyde threw them toward the back of the vehicle where the packs

28

and weapons were being passed in through the wide rear door.

"Not quite what I was after." Revell shrugged. "It's a mission more suited to a field security unit I'd have thought, but we're furthest forward in this sector so we got it. Seems a bunch of civies are trying to cross the Zone to reach the Russian lines . . ."

"That's a switch, ninety-nine percent of the traffic is the other way . . ."

". . . The word is they're a self-appointed peace mission, making a gesture for the world's press. If they do link up with the commies then the KGB's propaganda boys will have a field day. We're to grab them first, prevent it happening."

"Why not send in a squadron of air-cavalry," Burke's gruff disapproval floated from within the transport, "they'd soon locate the buggers, have them back within an hour. Save us a lot of pissing about."

Lifting his legs out to make room for their driver to take his seat, Revell jumped to the ground, landing beside Andrea. Now she was looking at him, and the same question was in her eyes.

"Could be the Soviets don't know they're coming; if that's the case we don't want to put on a big show that'll alert them. And if they do know about it, and we don't manage to catch the civies after mounting a maximum effort, then they'll capitalize on it all the more. So the approach is low key."

"And when, if, we find these . . ." Andrea sought the words, and finding them, filled their every syllable with loathing and hatred, ". . . these pathetic blinkered innocents, these Russian pawns, traitors, what then?"

"Kid gloves all the way. Orders are we're to gently turn them around and give them an escort back."

"You know the sort of people they will be, don't you." Andrea turned her contempt on Revell.

"I can guess. A worn-out union boss doing the last bit of harm he can before someone discovers he's been dipping into the pension fund, a member or two of the World Peace Committee or some other commie front organization, an elderly faggot from a respectable British university, and others on the same line, the usual assortment."

"And their leader, you know what he will be. A KGB operative, perhaps one who has been a sleeper for a long time. If you do stop them, bring them back, then what? I tell you, they will use their friends and contacts in the media to brand you a thug and a fascist, and they will bay for your blood. If you take them back, then you destroy yourself."

"What would you suggest. Put them against a wall and turn our rifles on them?"

"Why not. In the name of peace they would be pleased to see that happen to you, to all of us. In the name of peace, a communist dictated and dominated peace, such scum would be happy to see Russian tanks drive over the lawns of the White House, through the gates of Buckingham Palace."

If her concern for his fate had been prompted by affection, Revell would have been over the moon, but he was well aware that it wasn't. He found it difficult to understand her. A conscripted member of the East German Militia, when she'd deserted she'd chosen to hide among the human flotsam of a big refugee camp up north. She had even joined and eventually led a gang composed mostly of renegade East German border guards, the lowest of the low. At any time she could have escaped to the west, but hadn't until by chance she'd fallen in with the squad during their attack on those important Russian tank workshops.*

Her intense hatred of communism couldn't be the total explanation of her complex character. Revell's speculations, his attempts to predict her future behavior based on his observations were frequently confounded by some fresh contradictory act. If only he could get closer to her, get to know more about her . . .

"Ready to roll, Major." As he reported, Hyde made a point of stepping between the officer and the girl, to be sure of getting Revell's full attention. "We've run a check on the armament. The twenty-millimeter and co-axial machine gun in the turret are all right, but there's a fault in the remote control for the rear roof-mounted machine gun. It's nothing too serious though, we can probably fix it while we're on the move. What about the crates in the back? We're short of room, might be better if we unpacked whatever's in them."

"Electronic gear. Have Boris take care of it, that's his department. I just hope it works; we're going to need it, we're strictly on our own on this one. Now let's get moving, I've a gut feeling tells me the Reds are going to be looking for those civies as well, and they won't be wasting any time . . ."

*Zone 1, Hardtarget.

CHAPTER THREE

The hall was magnificent, as was every room in the Kremlin that Rozenkov had been led through, but the only feature of it that he took any real note of was the brilliant light from the many crystal chandeliers flooding into every corner of its vast interior.

It was a wry interest, founded only on a comparison of the lavish use of light bulbs here, and the difficulty he'd experienced in getting even a single forty-watt for his desk lamp at the Lubyanka, let alone the special electrical apparatus they'd been unable to obtain for the Intensive Treatment wing of the interrogation block.

He was not quite alone in that huge apartment. At its far end, flanking carved and inlaid double doors, were immaculate soldiers of the elite Kremlin Guard.

Rozenkov had done the best he could with his appearance, but he knew that when he passed between those two men he would by comparison be little better than a uniformed scarecrow. Their boots had walked no other surface than these highly polished floors, their jackets and trousers and caps had never been exposed to the elements. It was not security nor ceremony alone that put them there in that condition. The colonel recognized a contrived situation when he saw one; he should, he arranged enough for prisoners, in order to instill uncertainty, and inflict fear.

It was for the same reason, to over-awe and unsettle him, that he'd been ushered to the only chair in the surprisingly spartanly furnished Czarist showpiece. To stand would have betrayed nervousness, sitting removed the risk of giving that impression but meant his jacket would become creased, and so he sat forward, just a little, to keep his back from contact with the seat's elaborate embroidery.

Like chess, for every move there was a counter-move, and he was good at chess. Under pretense of smothering a slight cough with the back of his hand he glanced at his watch. One hour and forty-nine minutes. Not much of a wait set against the years he had spent working to get here.

The doors swung silently open. Colonel Yuri Nikolai Rozenkov stood, tugged straight the hem of his jacket and started forward. He realized he was sweating; he, who had killed a hundred men himself and signed away the lives of countless thousands more, he was experiencing fear.

As he approached and passed between them he could have sworn he saw the guards' blank expressions animate for the merest fraction of a second in sardonic smiles before instantly reverting to their previous immobility. They knew what he was going through. Rozenkov let his camera-sharp eye snap memory of them both and file the images in the "retribution pending" section of his mind. Should they ever find themselves within the reach of his power, he would take great satisfaction in prompting their recollection of this moment before making their lives unpleasant, and shorter.

There was more furniture in the side room. Much smaller than the hall, it was no less sumptuously decorated. If anything its ornamentation was a trifle richer, with gold leaf glinting from every corniche.

Eight men stood in a formal semi-circle in the center of the enormous Persian carpet that dominated the room. They in turn dominated it, in Rozenkov's eyes.

Several of the group were members of the Politburo, including two rumored contenders for the shortly to become vacant position of foreign minister, but senior among them was Ivan Forminski, a squat gorilla of a man whose political clout was the match of his reputed physical strength, and who was said, though only ever in whispers, to be within reach of the absolute pinnacle of power, the Presidency itself.

The stakes were suddenly much higher. At most Rozenkov had expected one, perhaps two tired old members of the Politburo, their presence padded by some of the rising stars from the Supreme Soviet, but this . . . If he read the signs correctly then there need be no limit to his ambition, the protegé of a man like Forminski could go on to anything. If the risks had become greater, the potential reward, the prospect of it, had grown in proportion.

For an instant he inwardly cursed his involuntary nervous hesitation as he stepped forward, then forced himself to calm down as he realized it had done him no harm. Men such as these expected others to fear them, expected such a reaction as their due and would most likely have been displeased had they felt they'd not made such an impression. It was Forminski himself who spoke.

"Comrade Colonel. It has been decided by a meeting of the Politburo, after consultation with the Main Military Council and the Central Committee of the Communist Party of the Soviet Union that you be appointed Head of Department A of the First Chief Directorate of The Committee for State Security. With the sudden . . . retirement of KGB General Khramoveski, for . . . health reasons, you are instructed to take charge of the department immediately."

Rozenkov had always imagined that this, what he had worked so hard and long for, would be the crown of all his efforts, but now he could dare to speculate where he might go from here. With Forminski taking an interest in him, the only limit to how high and fast he climbed was the speed with which that man rose above him . . . He had missed something . . . what was he saying . . .

". . . at the end of one month, if everything is to the satisfaction of the Central Committee you will then be confirmed in the appointment, with the rank of general . . ."

He was lucky, it was nothing vital, or was it?

". . . but in your case, Comrade Colonel, we are presented with a unique opportunity. A particular operation is in its early stages. It is a matter that will require careful, even delicate handling, but it is potentially a source of much valuable propaganda. An interest is taken at the very highest level. You will make it your first task, to the exclusion of all else. A rapid and successful conclusion would bring immediate confirmation of your new rank and position without need for further delay."

Careful to make sure his palm was dry, Rozenkov returned Forminski's grasp with the merest fraction less pressure. Each of the other formal salutes was as carefully calculated.

"Thank you, Comrades. You will find your trust well placed." Rozenkov had put many hours of deep consideration into the selection of those words; he was relieved to see that with them he appeared to have struck the correct balance between adequately expressing his gratitude at the honor being done him, and being brief.

As the doors glided shut behind him he experienced a sensation of surging relief pour through his whole body, and became aware at the same time of an urgent need to visit the lavatory. The tension had gone from him, and with it the shreds of fear, but his bladder and bowels kept record of their effect upon him.

A guide was waiting and led him from the building, pausing on the way to direct him with a silent gesture to a door discreetly tucked out of sight behind marble pillars where he never would have found it on his own. He only just made it in time. The paper was a soft pastel green tissue and he had to resist the temptation to take a spare roll from a shelf. That was a small indulgence he might be able to arrange for himself soon, the trappings of power in the Soviet Union sometimes took a bizarre form.

Absently Rozenkov returned the salutes of guards

and drivers as he waited for his car. He was not concerned with the architectural wonders of the palace about him; through his thoughts swarmed speculations as to what the important operation might be. Well, he would know soon enough, he would go directly to his new office. Forminski had said that an interest was taken in it at the highest level. No Russian, certainly no Moscovite, would have needed to apply any great amount of his inbred skill at reading between the lines to see the full implications of that simple sentence.

Whatever the operation, he was going to make it succeed. Nothing else mattered, that would be everything. Instant oblivion would be the happiest fate of anyone who stood in the way of his achieving that.

There were parts of the Zone that the war had never touched, and they were motoring through one such now. The Bavarian towns and villages they passed were intact, needing only a splash of fresh paint on the pretty houses to restore them as they had been a year before, when the war had threatened to turn this way and the population had been evacuated.

Some traffic on the roads and they would have come back to life immediately, but there wasn't going to be, and they wouldn't. Eventually their turn would come, the battles would swirl even through this remote corner of southern Germany and then for a few hours or days at most, the names of the towns and villages would be those mentioned in the world's press, and then as the war moved on they would slide back into obscurity.

By then they would have ceased to exist save as smoldering ruins with a few tracks bulldozed through them. Another year after that and even those who had once lived here would have trouble in finding the most memorable or distinctive of landmarks, as nature took advantage of the headstart destructive man had given her in finally reclaiming her territory.

"This wagon is a real bastard." Gradually Burke was learning how to cope with the Marder's peculiar handling characteristics, but already his arms ached from the strain of the constant corrections he had to make as the brakes, steering and suspension combined their faults to pull the vehicle to the left.

His complaint went unheard, as had all those before. Cotton from a first aid locker plugged the ears of those of the squad who didn't have headsets.

Clarence was one. Without a turret or remote controlled weapon to man he had wedged himself into an angle of the interior and concentrated on avoiding being jolted about the compartment. Occasionally an item of equipment that had been insecurely stowed, or a member of the squad who had relinquished a handhold at the wrong moment would bump into him. Inanimate objects he threw aside, bodies he fended off as best he could with the minimum of contact. He had to shout at the top of his voice to make himself heard to Revell, who stood with head and shoulders out of sight in the command cupola beside the turret.

"Can't we ease off on the speed? This old wreck just isn't fit for it."

"It's okay, we'll be slowing soon." Ducking down to mime the words to the sniper, Revell pushed his throat microphone closer to communicate with the driver. "There's a sharp right up ahead, take it."

The sheer bulk of the vehicle meant that several times they had to take to the side as they negotiated the narrow winding side road as it began to climb. Overgrown hedges were crushed beneath the churning tracks, and great lumps of bark torn from trees, fences and gates half hidden by the brambles and vines entwined about them were splintered and flattened into the soft ground.

Gradually the hill steepened, until their forward progress was little better than a walking pace. Not that it brought any diminution in the decibel level, that stayed high as the engine strained to move the twenty-eight tons of men and weapons and armor up the twenty-two percent gradient. Seven of the eight available gears had been used by the time they reached the top.

"I hope the fucking view was worth it." Dooley disentangled himself from ribbons of springy steel strip cut to open the packing cases. "For a shitty minute I thought we were going to have to get out and fucking push."

The rear door had to be opened manually when the hydraulics developed a leak and sprayed a high pressure jet of fluid at the floor. The others learned by Dooley's mistake when he slipped in the puddle, and stepped over it and him.

They'd stopped right on the brow of the hill, where a clearing gave them a panoramic view across the countryside. Dooley took one glance and then ignored it, choosing instead to concentrate on a detailed inventory of the contents of his pack to see if anything was missing after its several tumbling trips about the Marder's interior. He'd hardly begun when Sergeant Hyde ordered him to help the Russian unload the electronic apparatus.

Revell swept the ground below through binoculars. "This is useless, worse than trying to look for a needle in a haystack." Despite his pessimism, he kept quartering until in exasperation at the futility of trying to visually search mile upon mile of thickly wooded country, he switched to checking at random the few stretches of road that were visible.

A few towns and villages showed against the mass of gently undulating green, but the roads running through them were masked by the multi-story buildings. "Is that gadget working yet? It's our only hope."

"Ready, Major."

Faster than could have seemed possible with Dooley's assistance handicapping him, Boris had assembled the modules of the surveillance equipment and linked it by twin cables to a display tube and small control console he set on top of a stack of rotting fence posts. A final adjustment to the compact parabolic dish, supported by a thin legged tripod, aimed toward the low ground and then he activated the system. Immediately the self-checking circuits confirmed their condition by lighting a row of green bulbs below the screen.

"Do a magnetic sweep first." Revell watched the screen come alive with a thousand glowing dots. Though randomly sprinkled, several distinct clusters showed, and when he looked up he realized they corresponded with the positions of the towns and villages. Farms in particular showed clearly, as the sensors registered the metal of the corrugated steel sidings of barns, and large feed and grain silos.

"Try infra-red."

This time the whole screen came alive with color, but there were far fewer individual images. Against the dominant pink of the foliage, the soft white and pale blue of the concentrations of uninhabited buildings showed. In the middle distance a compact cluster of red dots had almost a pattern to their layout, while further away a solitary dark red trace was less sharp, fuzzily indistinct and pulsating.

"Radar now."

Again it was predominantly the metallic objects that registered, but it was more than that Revell was looking for. "Okay, shift back to IR again . . . now radar." There was no mistake, he'd read the screen correctly. "Got them." The lone distant trace was exactly the right size for a small vehicle without shielding around its engine or exhaust. With the picture rocking back and forth it became possible to see that the blurred infra-red image was like that because it alone of all those on the screen was moving, as the radar confirmed.

"Stay on it long enough to get an accurate fix and a plot of the route they're using, then dismantle this lot and get back on board as fast as you can."

"I think you should look at this, Major." Waiting until he had the officer's attention, Boris indicated the pattern-like cluster of traces. "These are interesting." He slid his finger across the bevelled glass surface of the screen to point to some of the other dark marks. "Most of these hot traces I can identify. If you use your binoculars you will see that they correspond with the positions of fuel storage tanks, or oil cooled electricity sub-stations, places that accumulate heat and hold on to it, so that they register more noticeably on infra-red, but these," he brought attention back to the pattern, "they are at the center of a patch of thick woodland, there is nothing there, no houses, no farms, nothing."

"Refugee camp? Cooking fires?"

"At first I thought so, yes, but watch when I rock the image between IR and magnetic."

The identical pattern showed in both modes. Revell didn't need to ask if the equipment was functioning correctly, he could see the row of low intensity hooded green lights for himself. "Only one thing that can be; it's the Russian battle group that's been rampaging around here. And they're right between us and those damned civilians."

"I've blown open too many of these tin cans to like the idea of doing my fighting from within one." Thorne had exchanged his cumbersome flamethrower for a compact Uzi sub-machine gun from the vehicle's own weapons rack.

"If this detour takes us around that gaggle of Soviet armor then we shan't have to." For once discarding his Enfield Enforcer sniper rifle, impractically long for use from the confines of the APC, Clarence had also helped himself to one of the stubby ugly Uzis, and prepared to use the sub-machine gun from the next hull side ball-mount to the sapper.

With the drive disengaged and the engine being run only to power the auxiliary systems, the Marder plunged down the hillside, carving its own path through the trees and undergrowth.

Masses of foliage were caught and churned by the tracks. Pliant branches whipped the hull as they were stripped of their leaves before being hurled aside. For a while the vegetation and flayed bark that wrapped itself about the return rollers and drive sprockets, and the rich leaf mold and loam adhering to the tracks almost silenced the din they had been producing.

That changed as they reached the bottom of the slope and Burke increased the revolutions of the idling six hundred horsepower engine, crashed through the gearbox to engage the drive and transformed the quiet burble of the exhaust into a raging bellow.

Their route lay cross country, the Marder taking every ditch and other obstacle in its stride, slackening speed only to cross embankment enclosed roads, where for a few brief yards the bare metal of the worn tracks would once more produce the maximum amount of noise as they pounded over asphalt.

From the vantage point of the command cupola Revell enjoyed three hundred and sixty degree vision, and he needed it when they broke from a belt of woodland into a series of rough fields lined with rows of seedling conifers. There was hardly any need for him to remind their driver to zig-zag. The Marder's erratic handling, combined with the yawing caused by the deep plough cut furrows of the rows, was in itself sufficient to make any enemy gunlayers task difficult.

A minute or two more and they would be crossing the Russian battle group's trail a mile to its rear. That should leave an adequate safety margin. Through his forward vision block Revell could make out the churned ground and broken hedges that marked the enemy armor's route.

They crossed the steel cut and crushed avenue and plunged into the gloom of the tall trees beyond. Instinctively Revell ducked as a branch smacked into the block. As he looked again they ran into trouble, literally.

CHAPTER FOUR

There was the thunder and shock of heavy collision as the Marder piled at full speed into the side of a Soviet scout car parked beneath camouflage netting.

It was no contest. The much lighter four wheeled vehicle was rammed aside with its armor crushed in, and caught a second time. As the APC charged past it slowly toppled over onto its roof, fuel spouting through rents in its plates.

"Keep your foot down."

Burke didn't need the major to tell him that, he'd have done it even if he hadn't seen the other components of the battle group's rear guard.

The range was point blank. Using the cannon's maximum depression Ripper had the tip of the slim barrel almost touching the turret of a Russian personnel carrier when he put a ten round burst into it.

With no chance to note the effect of the hits, they tore on. A spray of heavy caliber machine gun bullets whined off the turret and hull, instantly followed by a wild fusillade of cannon fire that brought down masses of leaves and branches on the Marder's roof. Another rapid burst was more accurate, one shell punched a hole clean through a road wheel and a second exploded on the turret front. Detonating among the bank of eight smoke dischargers, it tore some away, and ignited the grenades in others.

Smoke billowing from and over it, the Marder raced through the forest, chased by balls of green fire marking the tracer tails of armor-piercing rounds of larger caliber.

Ripper loosed a long burst in the direction of their source, but an accurate sighting of the tank from which they must have come was rendered impossible by the swirling white fog they involuntarily laid behind them, and its reinforcement of thick black smoke from a burning APC.

Fifteen minutes later, safely out of range, they stopped to take a bearing. Hyde could hear the crash and clatter of cannon and automatic fire continuing as the Russians vented mindless retaliation on the inoffensive trees. "If the civies have heard that commotion they'll be going like bats out hell. We'll have job catching them."

Reaching over their driver's shoulder, Revell activated the air conditioning to rid the compartment of fumes. Empty shell cases from the Uzis and the twenty millimeter rolled under his feet. "Most likely they did, but I'm pretty sure we'll get up to them. Even if whatever they're using has four wheel drive they're still near certain to stick to the roads all they can. We'll cut across country every chance we get and head them off."

"They sure can't have seen that commie battle group, otherwise they'd have gone straight to them, saved themselves a longer journey."

"You are an innocent, and a fool." Andrea didn't spare Ripper's feelings. "Whoever leads that delegation does not want to contact the first Warsaw Pact unit they happen to run into, especially not after having gone so short a distance. He is looking to make a grand gesture, and for that he must drag those with him all the way to the main Soviet defense line on the far side of the Zone."

Dooley dropped in through a roof hatch, into the rear of the compartment. He stank of smoke and the gloves he took off were singed and smoldering. "Don't I get some god-damned fucking awful jobs. It's taken me bloody ages to put out those shitty smoke candles. That hit made a right fucking mess of them, only a couple left that are still serviceable."

"You didn't put them out, it's impossible to smother phosphorus. All you did was wait until they'd near enough finished on their own and then kicked away the bits that were left."

"Oh yeah Mister Clever, and how do you reckon that?"

Not intimidated by the aggressive sneer, Thorne pointed to the big man's boots. "Well I got a clue from the fact that your feet are on fire."

Looking where the sapper had indicated, Dooley saw bright specks trapped in the seams and stitching around his toecaps. From each issued a thin streamer of white smoke. Prevented by a chorus of protest from the others from making use of the mouthful of spit he generated with sickening noises, he had to go out again and sit on the roof to pick at each piece of spontaneously burning chemical with the point of his bayonet. While he did it, he swore continuously as the heat and charred material discolored the mirror finish of the blade.

Examining their large scale map of southern Germany, Sergeant Hyde noticed that the several plots their Russian had made of the civilians' progress had been linked by a solid red line that continued in broken form as a projection of their expected course. "If our commie deserter's prediction is right, those civies must be completely out of their skulls. They're heading straight toward the most heavily chemically saturated and bug infested part of that contaminated territory. Do we go in after them, or wait on the fringes, knowing that poisonous toxin soup or a mob of bacteria are going to do our work for us?"

"They go in, we go in." Revell had already made his decision. "If they keep moving fast, and have a slice of luck, one or two of them might make it. Those lab bred germs work quickly, but the KGB disinformation experts will only want those civies in usable, not perfect condition. Even if they only survive an hour or two after their reception that'll be enough to give their Department A a field day. In that time they'll get all the footage they need. Best do a check on our NBC gear, I want us to be prepared if we have to go in."

"I did this morning. Regulations . . ."

"Just tell me the position. Is everyone fully equipped for operating under those sort of conditions?"

"No." It took an effort, went against his nature and training, but Hyde answered in the same abrupt manner the officer used.

"What do we need?"

"Eye pieces for the respirators, gauntlets, filter pads . . . It's this work we've been on. We haven't been using the suits but they've been taking a battering all the same." Bugger the major, he wasn't a bloody telex, he'd tell it his way. He wasn't about to leave a damn Yank officer with the impression he'd been neglecting his duty. "Being carted about, thrown in and out of transports . . . That microparticle-proof material can't take it for any length of time. I've put in for replacement items, but officially we've been non-combatant for a month, we're right at the bottom of the priority list."

"There's no time to go back and find a dump, requisition what we need. We'll have to patch and make do with what we've got, take our chances."

"You can count me out then." Burke had been listening with growing unease. "I've had to drive you lot into some bleeding stupid and dangerous messes, but I've never been expected to drive to me own funeral before. With the tear I've got in the hood of my suit I won't last above an hour."

"Another word and you're on a charge."

Burke declined to be put off by the NCO's threat. "So what? Order me in there and I won't be around to serve any time in the glasshouse. Damn it, all around here there's masses of places where the bloody Ruskies have dumped loads of chemical shit or bugs on other poor cruds. At least some of them must have had the right gear in good nick. If they copped a dose and tucked up their toes what ruddy chance do you think I've got?"

"Say that again?"

He pushed his luck past the limit with the sergeant,

but Burke felt rather differently about trying the same thing with the major. "Well . . . I was just saying . . ."

Rummaging in his map case, Revell wasn't listening. He sought something he'd thought they'd not be needing anymore, certainly not for a while and with luck never again. Pushed right to the bottom, the crumpling had not helped the grease and dirt stained special salvage map's clarity.

In seemingly haphazard fashion various color coded symbols had been superimposed on the snaking contour lines, roads, towns and villages. Some were grouped close together, other stood in total isolation. Having overcome the chart's almost willful attempts to defeat his efforts to fold it the way he wanted, Revell finally managed to bring the sheet to sensible proportions with their present location roughly at the center of the exposed portion.

The map had been given to him on the day they'd commenced their unpopular salvage work. Only a handful of symbols had been added to it since then, those marking the sites of the depredations of the raiding Russian battle group.

Each blob of color indicated the location of a past skirmish or battle, or where, in one of the rare air strikes in this part of the Zone, a convoy or mobile workshop or salvage detail had fallen prey to attack by fighter bombers seeking targets of opportunity.

The eastern edge of the map was shaded lime green, marking the boundary of the contaminated territory for which the civilians were heading. A faint echo of that bilious color surrounded some of the symbols elsewhere, including that closest to them.

"Look this one up, will you, sergeant."

It took Hyde a moment to find the relevant entry in the notes. As a possible candidate for salvage work the site was graded so low as to be near the bottom of the last page of the glossary. The information was cryptically brief, dismissing lives and events in three short sentences. Practice made it possible for him to garner more from those few lines than an inexperienced person would have thought possible.

"Not a nice one, Major. Cordoned area, suspected biological attack. A road gang, pioneers, went down without warning, to a man. Couple of field ambulances went in to mop up and they got clobbered to by whatever it was. Decontamination team followed, and when they went off the air the area was quarantined until it could be investigated."

Their NCO was right, it wasn't a nice one, not nice at all. So many ghastly new strains of bacteria and virus were being employed by the Russians to keep NATO on the hope that it was becoming possible to believe anything. Only a few months before, stories about a super bug capable of killing near instantly, even of finding a way to attack and destroy men as experienced and protected and prepared as medical and decontamination crews would have been utterly unthinkable, now it wasn't. And the isolated use of a new strain wasn't improbable either. The Russians' near indiscriminate use of chemical and biological weapons, even those whose potential lethality and risk was largely unknown, had brought a whole new meaning to the term "field trials."

It was a combination of the few vehicles involved, and the dangers attached to their recovery that prompted the site being classified so low in the list of priorities, but Revell saw the date of the incident when he glanced at the entry, and that changed a mind he'd thought already made up.

"This was four months back. If it is a bug, and there's no proof it is, then there's a fair chance it'll be neutralized by this time, otherwise the area would have expanded. The automatic sensors would have spotted it. A lot of the newer stuff has a short life. We'll have to take the chance. We need the equipment those trucks and ambulances will have on board." Leaning forward he pressed the engine starter button, and motioned Burke to drive, propping the map beside him. "That's where we're going first."

"Oh that's just fucking great, I get the chance to practice dying before having a go at the real thing." Though he spoke aloud, Burke took the precaution of switching off his throat microphone first, and the words were lost among the loud mechanical noises from the APC's engine, transmission and tracks as it accelerated.

Enough of the rest of the squad had overheard or been listening to the discussion for word to spread quickly. Without word having to be passed they began to put on the drab colored NBC suits and overshoes, pulling the draw strings tight at cuff and ankle. For the moment they left off the more restricting respirators, gloves and hoods, those of them who had them, but they kept them near, very near.

Resuming his place in the command cupola, next to their turret gunner, Revell kept watch as they entered close country. The road was hemmed in by dense forest on either side. Branches that overhung the road made a gloomy tunnel, at times making it so dark that he was tempted to turn on their white searchlight.

It needed little to prompt the imagination to run riot, conjure horrors, unseen dangers among the forbidding ranks of close set oaks and elms. At first Revell had been prepared to keep an open mind, heavily tempered by skepticism, on the question of what had killed the pioneers and their would-be rescuers. It could be that the information was no more than fanciful embroidery on an already embellished report that was perhaps in itself only cobbled together snippets from alarmist sources, but as they drove on he had to strive to keep the dictates of his common sense predominating over flights of fancy.

Damn it, it could be accurate. If the Russians had a super bug that could act so fast with one hundred percent fatal results, then they would not have confined its use to a single instance, and that against an unimportant road maintenance unit. But weird things happened in this war, and went on happening. And so did mistakes and gross errors of judgment, like the one that had led to the saturation use of chemical and biological munitions that had created the vast contaminated area the civilians were heading for.

The Russian commander who had used those means to rid himself of the problem refugees had first received a promotion and citation from Moscow for a job well done, and then when it had hit the headlines worldwide he'd become an unperson and had disappeared, doubtless to a strict regime labor camp, or medical experimental establishment.

Perhaps the elimination of the pioneers had been such a mistake, the premature use of a weapon being saved for greater things, or perhaps it had been a combat evaluation test that had been unsatisfactory and the Russian scientists had decided against its further employment. Whatever, they'd be there soon, and then they'd find out soon enough.

A red and white striped barrier pole was smashed and flung aside by the raked frontal armor of the Marder as it charged through the unmanned checkpoint. A faded warning notice was splintered beneath the tracks along with a rusted concertina of barbed wire.

They covered another kilometer before they came upon a second and far more substantial roadblock. A huge Faun six-wheeled truck was stopped broadside on across the entire width of the road.

"Stop here."

Already having slackened speed considerably in anticipation of the difficulty of negotiating the narrow gap between the tailboard of the truck and the big trees growing right to the road's edge, Burke had only to touch the brakes lightly to bring the Marder to rest a few yards short of the lane-straddling vehicle.

None of the APC's several automatic air sampling devices had detected anything approaching dangerous levels of pollution outside. Revell would have been surprised if they had. Most chemical agents could persist in their harmful state only a matter of hours after exposure to the atmosphere and the sun's ultra violet rays at this time of year. Had there been snow on the ground it might have been very different. Nerve agents like Soman, or VX could have been expected to remain lethal for weeks, in freak conditions even longer. But he could take no chances and had the others put on all their protective clothing before having the air conditioning turned to maximum.

He went out through the smallest top hatch, feeling the firm draft of the overpressure gusting past him as he did. Closing it after him he heard it being firmly locked from the inside.

Testing the short range radio link as he went, Revell walked to the truck. Passing its open back he saw that it was filled with drums of decontamination fluid, pumps and sprays, as well as bundles of body bags, a box of identification tags and a heap of unmarked wooden crosses.

Inside the respirator he was very conscious of the sound of his own breathing, and its magnified rasping and whistling filled his ears. He was sweating, and if the discomfort of the droplets trickling down the small of his back was not sufficient evidence, there were crescents of condensation forming at the tops of his lenses.

On the far side of the six-wheeler dark hummocky shapes lay scattered among the tufts of grass and clumps of weeds sprouting from the road surface. None of the bodies were more than a score of paces from the truck.

Double-checking the reading on the monitor attached to his belt, Revell confirmed its negative reaction with Hyde aboard the Marder before turning over the nearest of the corpses with his foot.

It moved easily, felt so light it seemed it could have no substance at all, only its filled-out shape betraying that there were the remains of a man inside it.

From deep within dark sockets shrivelled eyes

glared at him through the clouded lenses of a disintegrating respirator. As though it had waited for precisely that moment the perished rubberized fabric broke apart and an unnatural idiot grin, caused by the dehydrated flesh pulling drumskin tight over the skull, was fully exposed.

"No indication of the cause of death." Revell kept the transmit switch down on his radio. "Until it fell apart it looked like the suit was okay. Nothing suspicious in that, I think it'd just been out in the weather too long." He hadn't really been expecting to be able to determine the exact cause of death; at best he hoped to eliminate some possibilities and ascribe it to a general category. As he went to move away, to inspect another of the bodies he saw something he hadn't anticipated, something he hadn't even been looking for. Suddenly he realized why their instruments had failed to detect even a trace of residual contamination.

Reaching for the straps securing his respirator he began to pull it off. There was no point in wearing it any longer, it made no difference. No respirator would ever save him from what had killed these men.

CHAPTER FIVE

Gross had pestered and bullied Father Venables into changing places with him and now lounged forward to hang on the back of the front passenger seat. He let the tips of his pudgy fingers rest on the woman's shoulders, and occasionally deliberately stray from the quilted surface of her anorak to the bare nape of her neck.

"Will you get your wet paws off me, you fat slug."

"Oh, so sorry." Gross withdrew and slumped back into the rear seat. "I didn't realize you had such an abhorrence of physical contact. Those horny cheap porno films you made must have given me the wrong impression, mustn't they, Sherry. Sherry . . . Sherry Kane, that has to be a stage name, doesn't it. Did you change it to try and get away from your old clients, from when you were a ten dollar call-out model?"

It was Edwards who made the protest, getting in before the woman or the elderly priest, but he complained to the same person they would have, their driver.

Webb caught a glance of the old man in the rear view mirror, saw spittle fly from his misshapen mouth as he appealed for an authoritative voice that would curb the ex-union leader. Already he was tired of them all. They were not the traveling companions he would have chosen, but his KGB control in London had been adamant in guiding his choice. On a train he would have stood in the corridor rather than share a compartment with any of them. Kane with her tarty looks and shallow intellect, Venables with his pious innocence, Edwards with his overbearing air of superiority: and Gross, a physically repulsive man with a matching mind.

In an attempt to fill his thoughts with other things, he paid full attention to the road. Subtle but distinct changes were coming over the countryside through which they were driving. Autumn had not yet set in, but already many of the trees and hedgerows were losing their leaves. Even the needles of the evergreens had a life-leached and discolored appearance. The grass too had a prematurely wintery look, with the exception of few hardy weeds that maintained a healthy dark green hue, the turf of gardens and clearings being a sickly yellow shade, like it had been covered and kept from the sun overlong.

Webb noted, but wasn't alarmed by the unnatural transformation of the flora. This was the second time he'd tried to make this journey and in his previous, lone, attempt he had seen more violent, more ugly changes in the landscape.

Then he had been stopped by a full scale battle raging in his path. In the event it had proved to be a blessing in disguise. After the initial anger and disappointment he'd begun planning again, and recognizing, after his irate controller had forcibly pointed it out to him, the inherent weakness of acting alone, he'd enlisted the support of this diverse group.

"It looks pretty weird out there. Does fall come early here?" Sherry Kane pulled her jacket tight about her as she looked out on the withering foliage. "Are you sure it's safe to come this way?"

"Are you afraid of catching something that'll give you a rash and reduce your value between the sheets?" Gross watched her toss her head and flick at the ends of her hair without retorting. He longed to reach forward, slide his hand over her shoulder and inside her anorak. A good hard tug and he'd pull her tee-shirt from the top of her jeans, then drag the material up over her big breasts. His fingers would creep into the large cups of her bra and he'd squeeze those fat warm mounds hard, roll and twist her nipples until they became firm and jutting, then dig his nails into them until she screamed. Lovely.

In his creased and soiled trousers he felt the

coiled dampness of his fleshy penis stir sluggishly, short pulsing movements as it expanded toward full erection. He liked to feel it doing that, knew that soon, if he worked at the thought, it would start to leak. Oh lovely, really lovely, he was going to . . . oh it hadn't done that since he was a schoolboy, when the prefect had played with it in the showers, and afterwards he'd stood on his own in a corner of the locker room and watched the damp patch spread on his worsted shorts . . . The sensitive circumcised head of his penis was suddenly sticky, and his pants were wet . . . oh lovely.

Years of taking confession had instructed Father Venables in all the vices of man, and woman, and now helped him to disregard the vulgarity, the pettiness, that was displayed around him. Save for making an occasional protest when he heard the Lord's name being used as an epithet, and took extreme exception, he spent all of his time working on the speech he would make to the world press when they reached the Russian lines.

A balance had to be struck. His words would at once have to be an appeal for Christian love and forgiveness and peace, and a declaration of his faith in the basic honest intent of the Russians. But no matter what form of words he used, he found himself including every time a passage that would convey to his detractors back in Britain that his motives were pure, that he espoused no cause, favored no side.

For so very long he had worked for disarmament,

had spoken, marched, written, campaigned. He had borne the criticisms, said nothing when he had been called a tool of the communists, a dupe, a self-deceiving innocent, even when he had been labelled the Red Priest. At each accusation he had agonized, examined his position, his conscience, but each time he had come to the same conclusion. He simply could not believe that the communist leaders in the Soviet Union could truly be the totally evil men their reported actions indicated. There was good in all, they had only to be given the chance to show it and they would, he devoutly believed that . . . but still in all his public utterances there ran that thread of persistent apology. No, he must wipe it from his mind, what he was doing was right. He had prayed so hard for an opportunity such as this, he must make the most of it. There was some good in all men, there had to be . . .

Under its previous chief, Department A had been allowed to slide, become slack and inefficient, but it had not slipped so far, become so lax that its staff were unaware who the new man was to be. Rozenkov knew that his reputation would have gone before him. From the heads of sections down to the lowest filing clerk everyone would be waiting, poised to launch themselves into a make-believe of frenetic activity at the warning of his approach.

To get more than cosmetic results from the staff he had to do more than just walk in and take over.

For lasting improvements in the department's performance he would have to create an impression that even the dullest would understand as a clear warning that things were not going to be the same.

The security guard on the little used side door was half asleep over a crossword puzzle when the colonel entered, a state from which he was abruptly shaken when the legs of his chair were kicked away.

"You know who I am?" Rozenkov stood over the soldier.

"Yes, yes Comrade Colonel." He attempted to get up, but the officer stood on his fingers.

"Good. In precisely fifteen minutes you will report to the duty officer, and tell him you are under close arrest for a list of charges that will be supplied by me, later. Remember, fifteen minutes, if before then you move from here or do anything that might alert the rest of the building I shall personally take a hand in your punishment by returning and breaking many of the bones in your body."

As the door to a service stairway swung shut behind the colonel, the guard began to puke, violently and repeatedly. When all his stomach contents were used he went on heaving. He tried to pull himself up, but the racking spasms grew worse until he collapsed in writhing agony, the muscles of his stomach strained and ruptured.

Rozenkov's reign of terror had claimed a first victim.

The corridor serving the top floor was deep pile carpeted, and the suites of offices leading off exuded an air of luxury from their half open doors.

There was none of the usual tinny clatter from ill-made, worse maintained and worn out typewriters so typical of Moscow government offices; instead there was the muted chatter of near new Adlers and 3Ms. A computer terminal "tinged" an apologetic warning before smoothly disgorging a print-out.

Barging into the first room he happened upon, ignoring the indignantly imperious bleats from a plump breasted secretary, Rozenkov went to each highly polished desk in turn and swept every paper onto the floor. He treated four more offices in the same fashion, before coming to one even more opulent than the rest, that intuition told him had been prepared for his arrival.

Expensive, mostly western manufactured desk furniture shoved into a velvet covered waste paper basket, and after the hall-marked silver ink stands and onyx ashtrays went a pair of signed water colors of the Kremlin and Red Square from the wall behind the desk, and a group of bronzes from the top of a book case. As he might a bucket of swill, he hurled basket and contents into the corridor where they bounced from and made dents in the hessian covered panels on the wall.

The initial commotion caused by his violent arrival had brought many people from the sanctuary of their offices, but as confusion and surprise had been replaced by the shock of recognition, they'd disappeared faster than they'd materialized. Rozenkov let the ensuing silence hang for a long moment, before hitting every button on the inter-com simultaneously.

"I want every head of section in here now." He could imagine, but did not concern himself with the panic that simple announcement would have produced.

Those with an interest in who won, or lost, the race, extended far beyond the handful of individuals immediately concerned. All of the KGB staff in the department were career men, and all were aware, suddenly well aware, that their future could as easily be spent going rapidly down as steadily up. How they progressed in the service depended as much on the performance of their whole section as their individual performance and achievements. The section's results were principally judged by how well the section head operated, so there were many who waited in the lower levels of the building for first details to filter back down.

Hardly giving the men time to get into the room, let alone vie for position before him, Rozenkov wasted no time with preliminaries. He could be sure that some of the nervous men in front of his desk would not be fit for their jobs. Some would be stupid, some lazy, but there was not the time to replace them, and in any event he was certain that their deputies would be of similar stamp, chosen so as not to outshine their bosses. It would be a case of having to squeeze the best from them now, and later weeding those who could not take the pressure.

Indeed all of them would be on a form of

probation as far as Rozenkov was concerned. Those whose performance was adequate would be given longer to prove their worth, any of the staff who did not come up to the required standard would get no second chance, and in addition their names would go on a special list he intended to keep. If by their failure they caused him to fail, then his last act before his removal would be to ensure that he dragged them down with him.

"There is an operation underway that is of special interest to me . . ."

"I had anticipated that, Comrade Colonel . . . eh, Director . . . eh, Comrade Director. Full details are here."

His confusion and hesitancy over Rozenkov's proper title cost the head of operations much of the advantage he'd hoped to gain by his forethought and thoroughness. The remainder of it was lost when the summary page was ripped from the front of the bulky file, and the rest of it thrown back at him.

Hardly seeming to have glanced at the half page of double spaced lines, Rozenkov singled out the head of communications, identifying him by the radio-technical corps insignia on his shoulder.

"I want a radio link installed in here, on my desk, so that I can keep in personal touch with our units in the Zone."

"Of course Comrade Colonel." The head of communications smugly beamed as he avoided his discomforted colleague's mistake. "I can have you patched through on the army net. It will mean running cables through the building from the communication center in the basement, but . . ."

"I do not want to talk with army, not with corps, not division, not even battalion. I want to be able to talk direct with platoon and company commanders in the field. What technical problems may be involved I do not care. Have it done."

Glancing again at the summary, Rozenkov frowned, and there was a noticeable ripple of movement among the crowd, like a contagious shudder. "There is no mention of the arrangements for press coverage, why is that?"

"The intention is, Comrade Colonel, to fly the delegation to Moscow, to meet the representatives of the world media here."

It was only when she spoke that Rozenkov realized there was a woman in the group before him. Little beside the lack of shadow on her chin betrayed her. In a suit of very masculine cut, with a severe hairstyle, she was otherwise an unremarkable member. "And if we do that we lose half the value of the exercise. There must be no hint, no possibility of the suggestion being made that we brought them into the country via a neutral. A press conference we can arrange any day, an event, a genuine event, could be of propaganda value behind price. The press must be somewhere close at hand when we make contact with these civilians."

"But how Comrade Colonel . . ."

She was ugly, squat and ugly, Rozenkov found

time to wonder how a woman with no natural talent for her work could have got so high, without having had the advantage of attractive femininity to play on. Later he would learn more about her.

". . . that is a quiet sector. There is no reason for correspondents of the caliber we require to be there, what pretext could we give?"

"We shall select some unit within a short flying time of where we can anticipate the civilians making contact. If we tell the media people that the unit is to be inspected by the President of the Supreme Soviet, then they will be clamoring to go."

"With respect, Comrade Colonel, the foreign press have been speculating on the Comrade Leader's health. You will recall that they have made much of the fact that he has not been outside the Kremlin in six months."

"Then can you think of anything more likely to attract their interest and attention? There need be no embarrassment. Until they see him they will print nothing, and when the delegation appears instead they will take that as their story and forget the other. Now, what arrangements have been made for the civilians' interception?"

"All field units have been alerted . . ."

"Are you mad?" Rozenkov exploded. "Would you have them make contact first with a bunch of stupid Cossacks, or Serbs, who are either going to shoot them by mistake or bugger them and give them the pox? Order all units withdrawn from the immediate area, then get me the GRU liaison officer. Perhaps

Military Intelligence will have units in the vicinity that can cover for us until we are ready to airlift a Spetsnatz company into place."

Rozenkov was having to rebuild the whole operation from the ground up. Virtually nothing had been done, and what had was ill planned and uncoordinated. He was about to dismiss the gathering but checked himself, and lowering his voice so that they had to strain to hear every word, spelled out his position, and theirs.

"If this operation does not reach the successful conclusion expected of it by . . . by those above us, then there will be . . . changes . . . It should not need saying, but I do so to make everything clear; no excuses will be acceptable. The operation is basically simple, with only three component stages. That civilian delegation will be located, intercepted and used to the fullest advantage in the world press. It is possible, even likely that NATO troops will be used to prevent that happening. At all costs they will be stopped from interfering. Before they can do any harm to our plan they must be destroyed."

It took Revell only a minute to check the corpses of the remainder of the decontamination squad. In the suit of each he found the same neat circular punctures he had noticed in the first. Several of the bodies had been riddled, and it was very obvious that the men had walked into a hail of high velocity automatic fire.

With the Marder grinding and growling along behind him he started toward a pair of Landrover ambulances parked at the roadside a hundred yards on.

In each the crew of driver and medical attendant still sat in the cab, behind multiply starred windshields that were further obscured by splashes of congealed blood burst from gaping wounds caused by the deformed bullets' impacts.

A few yards further, and about a Bedford dump truck and trailer mounted compressor lay the rotting bodies of the pioneers who had been the original victims of the cleverly sprung Russian ambush.

Foxes and scavenging crows had torn open body cavities the snipers' bullets had not already pierced, and now past the stage of bloating putrefaction what was left of the skin and other tissue hung in ribbons from disjointed skeletons.

There wasn't the time to make a search and confirm it, but Revell knew that among the trees close by, investigation would have uncovered the spots where the carefully camouflaged riflemen had patiently lain in waiting for each arrival in turn. The trampled grass would have regrown, but the spent cartridge cases would still be there.

The Marder stopped by the ambulances and Sergeant Hyde began to organize the systematic looting of everything usable from the well equipped vehicles. Between them the Landrovers provided sufficient NBC equipment to make good all their shortages, and provide ample spares of those items most likely to need subsequent replacement under intensive use.

"You feeling a mite happier about going into those badlands now?"

Though he heard clearly over the intercom, Burke made no reply to their gunner. Instead he looked back to see if the American was still fidgeting in his turret seat as he usually did before resettling, and then engaged the drive fiercely. The violent tactic brought complaint from more than his intended victim.

"Fuck it, stop chucking this crate about like it was a fucking stock car." Pushing aside the avalanche of ammunition clips and medical kits that had followed him to the floor, Dooley regained his seat on the bench.

Boris had suffered worse than a sudden loss of dignity. Blood oozed from a deep gash high on his forehead, where his head had made hard contact with a hull fitting. He made no complaint, not even when Thorne, acting begrudgingly on their officer's orders, cleaned and covered the indented cut. No sound came from him when the hair the impact had embedded in his flesh was pulled away, nor when the first field dressing applied proved to be too small and had to be ripped off to be replaced by a larger.

"Tough buggers, those Ruskies." Watching, Dooley saw the deserter immediately resume what he had been doing, pausing only to wipe spots of blood from the respirator lens he'd been replacing.

"Maybe," Hyde didn't see it the same way, "or maybe they're just so damned thick they don't even know when they're hurt. I saw one of their field hospitals once, we over-ran it before they had a chance to scarper, surgeons were still working when we went in. That's if they were surgeons, I've seen apprentice butchers make a better job of carving meat. You should have seen it — crude wasn't the word. They might have a few fancy show-piece hospitals in Moscow, but for the poor sods they use as cannon fodder it's swab, stitch, splint and back into battle Ivan. The stupid sods line up like dumb animals to have their arms and legs lopped off without even an anesthetic. Our M.O. did his nut. You saw it Clarence, what did you think?"

"When I walked through the wards all I was thinking was what a lot of rotten marksmen there must be in the NATO armies. I've never seen so many gunshot wounds. In our casualty clearing stations better than three quarters of all cases are from mines and artillery. It was nearer fifty-fifty there, though that might have been because of the human wave tactics the Russians were using at the time. When there's a couple of thousand or more of the ugly swine coming at you, there isn't always the opportunity to take leisurely aim and go for a killing shot, it's a case of having to pump as much lead toward them as you can."

"I would like the chance to fire on such numbers." Andrea hugged her M16 across her chest.

"Killing them one by one will take so long." She looked pointedly at Boris, but he studiously avoided her eye.

He didn't catch all her words, but Revell could tell by her tone and expression that Andrea was talking about killing. Only rarely did she join in conversation, and then almost invariably on that subject. That alone should have made it easy for him to draw her on the subject of Inga.

After the circle of Russian armor around Hamburg had been broken he'd gone back into the city to search for her. All he'd found was her apartment block a blazing inferno and no sign of Inga. Those other residents he'd been able to find had told him little; shots had been heard, and a dark haired girl had been seen leaving shortly before the fire had broken out in Inga's rooms.

In a moment he could have set his mind at rest, or had his worst suspicions confirmed by asking Andrea what she knew, but either answer was too frightening to contemplate. One would have left him filled with doubt, the other would have tortured and torn his mind. And so he didn't ask, and instead of the single conflict that would have gnawed at his brain he was left with elements of both chasing through his thoughts and twisting and warping them until he didn't know what question to ask, what answer to hope for.

"We are behind them again." On an infra-red scan of the road ahead Boris had detected very faint, but positive, traces that revealed a vehicle had passed this way before them. "They have had the advantage of the delay of our detour. I would say they are at least an hour ahead of us, perhaps little more."

"And there are no more short cuts for a while," Burke eased back on the speed as he sensed a vibration setting in at maximum revs, "all we can do is hang on to their tails."

"So why don't we give up now. Whatever they're in it's obviously got the legs on this old rattle-trap." Thorne could see little save the blur of passing foliage through his own periscope, and was unsuccessful in persuading Dooley to surrender his place at a better sited vision device. "Those civies will be sitting down for a cozy vodka with a brace of commissars and a reporter from TASS while we're still frolicking about a couple of hours in their wake. Let's turn back and find a bit of fighting, somewhere I can find the chance to use this properly." He slapped the flamethrower's tanks.

"We go on, catch them even if it means we have to burst in on such a pleasant gathering." For a while Revell had been watching the condition of the surface of the road they were travelling. It was deteriorating rapidly. Long sections had been broken by frost. In places the edges had crumbled away and the further they went the greater became the profusion of storm-shattered branches littering it, and severed telephone wires and power cables draping it.

"These roads haven't seen traffic in a year or

more, and the blizzards last winter look to have brought down a lot of stuff. Sooner or later those civies are going to run into a blockage they can't drive through or around. Either that or they'll have to slow so often for lots of minor obstacles that we'll catch up to them that way. Whatever, we keep going."

Of course they'd keep going. Hyde had known what the officer was going to say. They always kept going, even when it didn't make any sort of sense, unless . . .

There was a loud clattering as hard fragments pummelled and sounded like they were threatening to penetrate the hull overhang. The left track was shedding the last of its ride cushioning, track-life prolonging rubber inserts. Even if it lasted long enough to take them all the way to the Russian lines, as they might have to, there was no chance it would bring them all the way back.

CHEMICAL AND BIOLOGICAL WEAPONS OF ALL TYPES WILL BE TREATED SIMPLY AS ANOTHER MUNITION AVAILABLE TO THE ARMY COMMANDER IN THE FIELD. IF CIRCUMSTANCES WARRANT IT, AND CONDITIONS ARE SUITABLE, TOXINS, NERVE GASSES, BLISTERING AND BLOOD AGENTS, BACTERIAL AND VIRAL WEAPONS WILL BE USED.

IT SHOULD BE KEPT IN MIND THAT THE THREAT OR FEAR OF THE USE OF THESE WEAPONS CAN OFTEN SERVE AS EFFECTIVELY AS THEIR ACTUAL EMPLOY-

MENT. THE OSTENTATIOUS MOVEMENT OF CHEMICAL TROOPS INTO FORWARD AREAS, THE CONSTRUCTION OF DUMMY HANDLING FACILITIES AND DUMPS; ALL THOSE WILL HELP TO FEED FALSE INTELLIGENCE INFORMATION TO THE ENEMY AND ENCOURAGE THE INCORRECT INTERPRETATION OF THAT HE ALREADY HAS. THE SKILLFUL COMMANDER WILL NOT NEGLECT THE USE OF AGENTS AND SYMPATHIZERS TO SPREAD ALARM AMONG THE CIVILIAN POPULATION BEHIND THE ENEMIES LINES, AND EVEN AMONG HIS BATTLE FORMATIONS.

SUCH MEASURES WILL FORCE THE ENEMY TO DE-GRADE HIS FIGHTING ABILITY BY TAKING ALL PRECAU-TIONS, WHILE LEAVING OUR OWN TROOPS FREE OF ANY SUCH CONSTRAINTS.

From a Russian Army manual (Written and published 1969, revised 1972/75/78/80/82) used at Staff Officers college 12, and considered by western intelligence to be the Soviet military's standard work on the subject.

CHAPTER SIX

The tree had brought down telephone lines, and the thick tangle of wires combined with the jutting splintered timber to form a barrier the Rangerover could not bulldoze its way through.

"That's it, give it a good swing." Having deliberately given the woman the axe, Gross watched her heavy breasts jiggling against each other as they threatened to pop from the restraints of her brassiere.

"Stuff it, you pervert, that's the only tool you'll ever be any good with."

Trying with a lop-sided drooling grin to conceal his annoyance, Gross set to work with the wire cutters, but he felt the color rising to his cheeks all the same. He'd get his own back for that, he'd find a way. Maybe he'd catch her bending, and shove his cock up her big bum, just to hear her beg him to stop, or at least use vaseline. Or perhaps he'd thrust it into her mouth, in and out, in and out, and have her milk him till she choked on the squirting product of his massive orgasm. Oh he knew he could do lots with her that way, gallons and gallons . . .

Father Venables hovered about the front of the

Rover, at times looking as if he might take up a spare implement and assist, but then his fluttering hand movements would cease and he'd clasp them behind his back and once more content himself with just making noises of encouragement, and occasional half gestures of applause for their efforts as gradually the obstruction was chopped out and pushed aside.

Only Professor Edwards remained in the vehicle. From a green plastic Harrods carrier bag he took a flask and carefully poured a cup of beef soup. A crinkled parcel of aluminum foil he unwrapped to remove a buttered water biscuit, carefully rewrapping and stowing the remaining four back in the bag.

"How nice, oh how very nice." Gross stuck his head in through the rear window and his sweat dripped onto the seat. "Am I invited, or is this a private picnic?"

"This is just to keep my strength up. Of course I would help you all if I could, but I have this condition . . ."

"Such a pity."

"I do not feel you are offering genuine sympathy, but if I should have misinterpreted your tone, then thank you. It is nothing too serious you understand, but my specialist has told me I must take care, not indulge in undue exertion. And so you see, much as I would love to assist . . ."

"You always shop there?" With a moss-stained, stub-nailed finger Gross prodded the gold print on the carrier.

"Do I . . . ? Oh, I see. Well, yes, actually, I do pop in on occasion, when I'm in town, and of course I have a hamper at Christmas, just for a treat."

"Went there once myself. Took my kids to show them where the nobs did their shopping. We had afternoon tea there, only one of my girls dropped her yogurt under the table, and went looking for it. Sort of upset some of the old ladies making their monthly pilgrimage."

"So I can imagine." Pretending total absorption with his scanty meal, Edwards kept his head down until the fat man lost interest in watching him alternately nibble and sip. He watched the retreating union leader's back. Their mission had forced strange and distasteful company on him. Not one of them would have come within a thousand years of receiving an invitation to his college's high table, and he could not see a place for them in the new order of things, when socialist revolution swept Britain, as surely it must one day soon. There could be no seat for them among the vanguard of the proletariat who would herald and guide in the start of the new age. Sipping the hot peppery soup he bathed in the visions that had sustained his spirit and nourished his intellect since his first days at university, since he'd become a member of the apostles . . .

Fuck. Sherry Kane glanced about to see that no one was looking, then wrenched at her right breast. One of the damned wires was shifting again, threatening to come jutting out through the thin material of her sweatshirt like a god-damned radio antenna. First chance she got she'd take it off. She'd just have to take care with camera angles when they reached the end of their journey, make sure none of those hick Russian photographers made her look like they sagged to her waist.

81

As she wielded the axe she could feel blisters raising on her palms, at the base of each finger. It was strange though, despite the obnoxious attentions of Gross, despite the unexpected exertion and the dishevelment it brought, she was kind of enjoying herself.

Just why was hard to figure. She just felt sort of, well elated, real happy. Maybe it was because at last she was going to grab all the headlines, maybe because using the axe it reminded her of when she was a kid, when her only worry was being left alone with Uncle Harry, when he used to pull up her nightdress and rub against her, but that apart all had been well with her world.

All was going to be well with her world again. When they reached the Russian lines the gamble she had taken, the risks of short term unpopularity with the audience and the studios back home, all that would be wiped away. Within a week she'd be bigger than Fonda, bigger than anybody. Swinging the work brightened blade high she brought it down hard and severed the branch she'd been working on.

In the unaccustomed physical exertion Sir Julian Webb found an outlet for his irritation at the delay, and also a release for some of the pent-up anger with life in general that seethed inside him. It was that incident the day before he'd left from Heathrow, when he'd returned to his rooms in Chelsea a little earlier than usual, and found Raymond with that pimply paper-boy.

Never a voyeur, only ever a participant of the homosexual act, he'd been struck by the vulgar ugliness of it all, on finding Raymond standing with a jar of vaseline in one hand, and his stub of an erection in the other, trying to fit the lubricated organ into the youth's tightly rounded pink backside.

The scene stuck in his mind; the youth's soiled pants tangled among the patched jeans around his ankles, the resigned look of boredom on his acne etched features, the crumpled five pound note clenched hard in his fist: and Raymond, his plump face red with excitement and anticipation, mouthing crude obscenities to encourage the boy and prepare himself.

It was not Raymond's betrayal of their thirty year relationship that had hurt; it had not been active, had hardly been affectionate for a long time. No, it was whom he chose to do it with. Had he known about him and the youth? Webb could hardly believe it, Raymond had been away the week he had . . . when the youth had come in for a drink of tea. The flushed thrill of that first accidental brushed contact was with him still. Every action of the youth's had been so obvious, so blatant a come-on . . . It had been the youth's greed for money that had frightened him into ending the tawdry affair before Raymond's return, and in all truth he'd not been sorry. After that first time he'd not really enjoyed it. Perhaps he was getting old, perhaps he was just old fashioned, but the act had been so casual, so bereft of any . . . romance . . . that the mechanics of intimacy had not been sufficient alone to make him want to continue the relationship.

Any last lingering doubts he'd had as to whether or not to make this trip had been cast aside at that moment when he'd walked in and caught them . . .

"I'm absolutely fucking knackered." Gross straightened and put a hand to his aching back. "That bloody bus must have the guts to shove aside what's left. For Christ's sake give it another go."

"Wait, wait. Before we go on . . ." Father Venables experienced an all too familiar sensation, and trying hard not to look as if he was clutching himself, shuffled off the road and a little way into the straggling undergrowth that bordered it. "Ah . . ." That was good. He had adjusted his clothing only just in time. Really, this condition was too unfortunate, too embarrassing. Possibly it would help if he reduced his fluid intake.

He coughed at the slight irritation caused by dust-like wisps that rose from a fungi covered rotting log his dark colored urine hosed across. Fastening the last of his buttons before starting back, as he pushed through the pliant branches he felt a curious tingling sensation throughout his body, but particularly so about his lips and ear lobes and fingertips.

"Would you be so kind as to assist me." Curious, he had to ask Professor Edwards for help to climb back into the Rangerover. How strange, really he felt very weak . . . no, not weak, it was rather a numbness that rapidly emerged into a will sapping, strength draining fatigue. Most peculiar, he couldn't imagine what was wrong with him, he hadn't had a cold in years, yet this was like the fast onset of the symptoms of virulent influenza. Ridiculous though, it couldn't manifest itself so quickly, not from ordinary causes . . . ordinary causes . . . this was no ordinary place, this was no ordinary virus, perhaps it was no virus at all.

Now there was a, not a tightness, more a definite slackness in his chest. As the Rover robustly bulldozed the near branchless trunk of the tree aside, and they got under way once more, he realized that breathing was becoming increasingly difficult.

"Oh dear me no, oh now now, oh please not now, I have so much still to do."

"What's the pee stained old fool on about?" Crowding in, Gross didn't bother to look at his elderly companions on the rear seat, but when Venables spoke he became aware of the priest's blanched face and shallow rasping breaths. "You caught yourself in your trouser zip?"

Struggling, and exerting himself to do so, Father Venables managed to slur five more words, "Dear God, I forgive them," then locked his grip on his rosary as paralysis raced through his body to rob him of the ability to say or do more. He could no longer move, not even to cross himself.

"Is he having a stroke?" Sherry Kane turned to look into the back and couldn't believe it when she saw the other two not helping, but actually trying to distance themselves from the old priest. "Say what kind of creeps are you, at least loosen his collar, he ain't hardly breathing." She reached out to do it herself, but Gross lunged to grab her wrists before she could.

"Don't touch him. That isn't the battery in his pacemaker going on the blink, he must have picked up something when he went off on his own."

"What can we do?" The handkerchief Edwards wadded over his mouth as he squeezed himself into an extreme corner not caring that his actions clearly indicated to all that his concern was more with avoiding whatever might be affecting Venables, than helping to apply some remedy. "Can he pass it to us?"

"I don't know about the rest of you, but I'm not going to give him the fucking chance. Stop the car." Even before the Rover came to a halt Gross had the door open and was jumping out. From the side of the road he picked up a moss covered bough and using it as a giant prod, began to push the dying man from the vehicle.

Giving a frightened yelp as he realized that Venables was being shoved toward him, Edwards made a hasty exit from the far door and got clear just in time as the priest topped out onto the road.

Unable to resist, Venables had to suffer the pain of the rough wood rammed fiercely into his side and could do nothing to prevent arrest or soften his fall when the seat was no longer beneath him. Without being able to even put out a hand, he struck the road face first, hard, doing a flopping half roll before coming to rest against the shallow grass bank at the roadside. His glasses had broken and blood poured from cuts about his eyes and from his burst nose.

But pain, even that of the shard that had pierced his right eyeball, was fast becoming a distant thing. What vision he had left was dimming, and his thoughts were blurred, running together and losing their meaning like the images and colors of a painting dissolving in the rain. The last sight he had before it went altogether was of Professor Edwards splashing large quantities of disinfectant over the seat before jumping aboard the already moving vehicle.

The feeble beating of his heart and the sound of shallow breaths whistling past the broken dentures lodged in his throat were the only sensations he was aware of, and his oxygen starved brain never registered the instant when they ceased.

Only Webb did not join in the exchange of accusation, excuse and argument. His only feeling over the event was contempt for them all. It was a mark of how little regard any of them had for each other that the discussion centered not on the fact that a dying man had been jettisoned to a suffering lonely death, but around the moral issues involved.

He listened as the passion and anger flowed back and forth. Gross and the woman made the most noise, but the union-leader's prime concern was justifying his actions, while Kane's contribution, though equally loud, was an intellectually lightweight mishmash of half remembered and less understood quotes from schoolroom Marxist pamphlets.

When Gross made an occasional interjection it was usually drowned by the shouting, or interrupted repeatedly, and then he would scowl and his wrinkled face would gain another set of creases and his sharp eyes would narrow and project his hatred and frustration.

A point was reached where it appeared likely that blows would soon be struck. Kane's voice was so shrill she seemed at times to go off the audible scale and Gross was purple, with his every word accompanied by a shower of spittle. Of the trio the professor alone seemed to have retained a degree of self control, but he sat with tight lipped bridled silence that had all the menace of a volcano on the verge of violent eruption.

Reluctantly Webb framed a comment to take the heat from the situation, but he never needed to utter it. Circumstances intervened.

On the road ahead was a small crowd of a dozen or so civilians. When they saw the Rangerover coming they made no move to step aside, instead they fanned out across both lanes and linked arms to form a human barrier.

Absorbed in the violent discussion, Sherry didn't see the group until she turned back to the front to discover why they were slowing. They looked strange, she blinked and looked again, still she couldn't make sense of what she saw, it was like she was seeing images in a grotesquely distorting mirror.

The people rushed forward to crowd about the vehicle, and it was as they tried to reach in through the open window, as they came so close that Sherry could feel their breath on her cheek, that her brain could no longer block the truth of what she could see.

She saw the bare flesh of their hands and arms and faces, those terrible, terrible faces, and started to scream; and went on screaming as with balled fists pressed savagely hard into her eyes she tried to hide from a sight she wished she had never seen.

"He was still alive when they left him." Sergeant Hyde made his inspection of the body from a safe distance. "Look at the state of him. He must have lost the best part of a pint of blood from those facial injuries, but there's no sign of a dressing, nothing.

They dumped the poor old devil."

"Could have fallen out I suppose, it might have been an accident." By his feet Thorne had noticed smears of blood and fragments of glass.

"They'd only just pulled past that tree, they couldn't have been doing any speed, certainly not enough to kill him. And if that were the case, why go off and leave him. No, judging by the marks on his face I'd say he was thrown out, probably because he suddenly developed symptoms that scared the living daylights out of them."

"So that kinda proves this place is still pretty lethal." With a long stick that lay nearby, Ripper gave the corpse an exploratory prod. "How come back in the US we were told all that chemical crap only lasted a mite longer than a month at most, and then it weren't dangerous no more. There ain't been no action in these parts for better than half a year, so it ought to be safe hereabouts, or was that just bullshit they gave us at boot camp?"

There were no indications of vomiting or diarrhea on the body, and Revell could see no signs of burning or blistering either, but he knew that some chemical agent had to be the cause of death. Even with the enhanced incubation periods possessed by many of the latest strains of biological weapons, no virus or bacteria could possibly have acted so fast. "They told you right, but it's been found that some toxins can be absorbed by certain plants, and give off again later, a lot later. The old fellow must have gone off for a pee and found that out for himself."

"Oh that's great." Dooley moved his foot from a nettle rooted in the cracked road surface. "Ain't enough we've got to watch for boards warning of minefields. Now we got to keep an eye open for 'keep off the grass' signs."

They were reboarding when they saw the refugees coming. The group moved slowly, and four of them held the handles of a roughly made litter. Hesitating when they saw the armored personnel carrier, after a hurried whispered consultation among themselves they came on, very slowly.

"Where can they have come from?"

"Doesn't matter." Hyde shoved the Russian toward the APC, as the major urged the others to board quickly. "The last thing we need is to get involved with a bunch of refugees."

Instructing their driver to take them forward cautiously, Revell had to order a dead stop when the group deliberately spread across the width of the road to block it. Standing half out of the top hatch he looked at them, and couldn't prevent a shudder.

He'd been expecting something bad, but even so was not sufficiently prepared for their appalling condition. Ragged clothes, bare bleeding feet and running sores he'd seen before, they were as much a part of the refugee scene in the Zone as hunger and dirt, but the appearance of these . . . creatures, was hideously grotesque in the extreme.

Huge boils distorted the shape of their faces, and their hands and arms were swollen and misshapen by clusters of more of the same. Two children among the group had thick bandages bound over their eyes, but still kept their heads low and with hands covered by a livid rash shaded their similarly afflicted faces.

Improvised splints were lashed tight about the legs

90

of the young woman on the stretcher, and where her bare flesh showed between the windings of torn cotton it displayed disfiguring black spots.

A man came to the side of the Marder, and through the evident pain of talking, an effort that opened the distended tissue surrounding his mouth and caused a mess of blood and pus to drop from his chin, spoke to the major.

"Will you help us please. I beg you."

He had to pause, swaying as if close to the limit of his tolerance of the agony he was enduring.

"Please, please help us. The others would not listen, they drove straight at us." He indicated the figure on the stretcher. "My wife is hurt. You must help us."

Thorne had come up beside the officer. He winced at the sight of the refugees, and spoke quietly to the major from behind the cover of a hand cupped over his mouth. "They're as good as dead. We were always expecting the commies to use stuff like this against us in Hamburg. They never did, but I got to learn all the symptoms. Most of the adults have got anthrax, and they've got it bad. The kids have got San Paulo fever, or something like that. See the rash? And they can't stand the light. Not sure about the woman on the stretcher, could be plague of some kind, but it looks like it's in the terminal stage."

"I'm sorry, we have to go on." Revell hardly needed the information from the sapper. He'd identified the anthrax for himself, and had made intelligent guesses of the other diseases. "All we can do is leave you food and medicine. I have to maintain radio silence at present, but I'll call ambulances and a medical evac team as soon as I can."

The spokesman shook his head. His first words came out as animal noises and he had to stop, summon reserves of strength and try again.

"No, that is what we want." Slowly he lifted his arm and his tattered sleeve slid back to display even larger blisters on his forearm, so close together that in overlapping masses they doubled the thickness of the limb.

As the refugee's wavering finger indicated the 20mm cannon, Revell slowly and carefully let his hand slide down to fasten on the butt of his pistol. These didn't look the sort, weren't in the condition to be active bandits on the look-out for weapons and transport, but he had to be ready for anything. Staying silent on the demand he waited for the man to speak again.

"Please, do not misunderstand." He brought his hands together in a gesture of supplication but his bloated fingers would not enmesh and so he put them as close as their deformity would allow. "Please, I am asking you to kill us."

CHAPTER SEVEN

Had there been time to do it thoroughly, Colonel Rozenkov would have enjoyed breaking in his new command, but the operation came first and until it was over there would be no chance to commence so pleasant a task, and savor it.

His arrival had produced an effect in the headquarters of Department A that could be compared with the trauma experienced among the ordered lives of termites on their mound being suddenly and violently ripped apart. Circumstances were forcing him to use sledgehammer tactics where he would have preferred the scalpel. Both achieved the same result, the same bloodletting, but it would have been better done in a manner that had let him keep close control of every cut, every transplant, every amputation. The precision of surgery was much his favorite method.

But heavy handed tactics did have the virtue of bringing quickly to his notice weaknesses in the organization that might otherwise have escaped his attention for days or even weeks. Already four members of the staff were under arrest. Two of them did not even know it yet. Armed escorts were on the way to fetch them now, from whatever pastime, girl friend or other distraction it was that kept them away when they should have been on duty.

He had almost forgotten, there was a fifth arrest, it had been right here, in his office. The woman had been stupid, the moment she had obviously non-accidentally brushed her big breasts against him it was clear how she had risen to the rank of lieutenant. In her haste to be the first to try to ingratiate herself, perhaps to ensure the security of her position, or possibly to gain further promotion she had acted too soon. Stupid sow, she should have waited, appraised him first. Most likely the result of her advance would have been the same, but at least this way she had got to know immediately what new position he had in mind for her.

In essence it was not dissimilar to what she'd been trying for, but it would be in neither the place or the circumstances she'd been aiming for.

Spreadeagled and manacled across a stained, nail raked rough table, the instrument between her legs would be an electrode, not his.

In earlier days he had always personally supervised the questioning of the more attractive women. That was the sole indulgence, the single luxury he permitted himself. A refinement he had introduced was to force females to drink copiously beforehand, and then watch the dramatically enhanced effect of the treatment when they could no longer control their bladders.

And there was something else, the private thing he did when the others had gone and he was alone with his . . . subject. He could admit, to himself, that he was tempted by the lieutenant's fat udders. They would have made good hand holds as he thrust in and out.

Others would have that pleasure, he could not. He would be under close scrutiny in the first few months he was here, until he weeded out those who might be tempted to be disloyal to him. Before his purge was complete, by demotions and blocked promotions he would make many enemies among the staff. A few would, with cause, hate him so much that their fear of him would not over-ride it. Until he identified those people, and removed them, he would have to go by the book, to the very letter.

The abrupt, almost peremptory double knock at the door came at virtually the instant it started to open. An immaculately uniformed officer from military intelligence entered briskly and walking to the desk threw a salute that in its starkly contrasting slackness was tantamount to insolence.

"I see that you are not overawed in my presence, eh . . . ?"

"Major Morkov, Comrade Colonel."

There was a shade more difference in the words than there had been in the salute. Rozenkov knew he had caught the man off guard by being so blunt.

"Some commanders might think that a good thing, healthy. You are married, Major? With a family?"

Following the first, that question was not what he'd been expecting, and the major rapidly regained the attitude he'd displayed when he entered. Obviously the new boss of Department A was an old fool who had achieved his promotion through contacts, not by merit, if he was prepared to waste time engaging in trivial conversation. It would be as easy dealing with this one as it had with the last weakling. And to think that for a while he had been worrying about the change-over. He saw now that his post as GRU liaison officer would remain as comfortable and undemanding as before. Still, it might not hurt to humor the old fool.

"Yes, with three fine sons."

"How nice for you. I feel I should tell you though, that you will never see them again if your attitude is not transformed instantly into apologetic grovelling compliance with my every wish and whim."

"I . . . I . . . Comrade . . . I am an officer under the command of military intelligence, I report directly to the chief of the GRU."

"Who happens to be General Anatoli Mischenko. You must know that the head of the GRU is always an ex-KGB officer. Anatoli is an old friend of mine, owes me many favors. Should you disappear without a trace I have only to ask him to believe that I have no knowledge of what has happened to you, and that will be an end of the matter, as it will be of you. It may be that you are under his command, but you are under my roof. I do not doubt that in this vast building I could find a room where you could be kept half alive for a very long time."

"Yes, Comrade Colonel."

The salute that accompanied the trembling words was immaculate, spoiled only by the terrified man's inability to entirely prevent his hand from shaking.

"Good, we understand each other. Here is what I want." Rozenkov threw a rolled map across the desk to a fumbling catch. "On there is marked the probable route being taken by a group of western civilians I am anxious should cross the Zone unmolested, by NATO troops at all, by any of ours until we have a proper reception prepared for them. Already I have a report that a squad of enemy troops are in close pursuit. You will employ any men you have available in the area to intercept and eliminate them."

"I understand, Comrade Colonel."

"Splendid, your continued robust health and contentment with family life depend upon it. Remember, on no account are the civilians to be stopped, they must not even know we are taking an interest in them at this stage. Do whatever you have to, you know the results I require." Rozenkov farted loud and long, the pressure of the escaping gas near lifting him in his chair. "Here, you may sit at my desk, use my radio link. I have to go for a shit."

As he left the room, and the overpowering stench behind him, Rozenkov enjoyed a sardonic inward laugh. There was an apt symbolism in the pungent fumes the major was having to endure without protest. The men he would be ordering into action would be coming up against gasses themselves. Instead of stinking bowels though, they might smell faintly of fruit or apple blossom, or new mown hay, but for all their fragrance they would be utterly deadly.

Sitting down he noticed with satisfaction that the paper was a roll of decent quality tissue, not the usual box of glazed individual leaves. For the first time since he had entered the building he had a moment to think. On reflection he was beginning to see certain advantages in some of the improvisations that urgency had forced on him. Principal among them was what he'd most recently arranged.

The employment of GRU units for much of the dirty work could turn out to be a really good thing. He would hold his own men back until the interception could be made with maximum effect, letting military intelligence take the casualties, and if anything went wrong, a large share of the responsibility. Yes, it was a good arrangement.

By now the liaison officer would have examined the map, seen where he was having to deploy his troops. For him, and for them, it would not be a good arrangement. He would have trouble explaining their use to his superior, and their loss.

On two occasions in the past Revell had been forced by circumstances to finish off, to kill, members of his own command who were desperately wounded and in danger of falling into Russian hands. That it had been by far the most humane thing to do, saving them from the further agonies of torture; that had not made it any easier. What the leader of the refugees was asking was no more palatable.

He knew he could not do it himself, nor could he order any of the others to do it. Asking for a volunteer was no solution either. Almost certainly Andrea would be the only one to do so. His mind was already in sufficient turmoil over her for him not to want to carry an image of her gunning down unarmed sick refugees, whatever their condition, how ever great a mercy it might be. He sought another way.

"Dooley, up here, bring your pack. Not that one,

the one you keep tucked out of sight."

Slowly and suspiciously Dooley produced it and handed it to the officer. He watched nervously as the major rummaged about inside it.

Various small tins and boxes were crammed into the bulging pack and Revell had to delve deep before he found what he wanted. The Soviet Makarov pistol was wrapped in a piece of garish printed cotton, along with two loaded magazines. Throwing the hand gun to the spokesman, he retained the clips for the moment.

"You know how to use it?"

"Yes." Slowly and painfully he tested the action, noticed it was unloaded and looked back to Revell.

"I'll drop these off a little way up the road. You understand why, don't you?"

"All we want is to die, to end our suffering. There is no anger left in us, not even toward the Russians who made us this way. We are past caring. An act of indiscriminate revenge upon you would serve no purpose."

"I'm sorry . . ." Rebinding the cloth about the magazines Revell tossed them down.

"Thank you." Fumbling with fingers made clumsy by disease-induced deformity he slid a clip into the butt, and turning his back on the Marder shuffled toward the children who sat by the side of the stretcher.

Without being ordered, Burke eased in the drive and made the quietest departure he had achieved to date. As the hatches were being pulled shut they heard a shot. A second followed before they were secured.

* * *

Speed was reduced to a crawl, with the APC in bottom gear as they approached the summit of the long climb, when a pin sheared and the left track broke. At that slow pace their driver was able to bring the machine to a halt before they ran off it.

Following the sergeant from the Marder, Revell joined him in an inspection of the damage. "Could have been worse, at least we won't have to piece it, but it's another hold-up we could have done without."

"About thirty minutes I should think, Major. Less if the broken pin comes out easily."

"They never fucking do." With the maximum amount of noise Dooley dropped the tool kit.

Boris and Thorne struggled with a spare track plate that was proving difficult to remove from the brackets fastening it to the hull side. Their comments as Burke sauntered past carrying a single track pin, and grumbling about having to do it, were drowned by the thunder of Dooley's assault on a recalcitrant fragment of distorted metal still retaining the failed component.

"Post a guard sergeant, and have an air-watch kept, then we'll have a stroll to the top and see what lies ahead. Might as well take that advantage of this stop."

The view was not as panoramic as that they'd had from the hill on which they made their electronic sweep, but it was even more informative. Before commencing a systematic search of the slice of Bavaria laid out before them, Revell couldn't resist a swift

100

general sweep along the road where it went off into the distance.

"Got them." Studying the scene a moment longer, he handed the binoculars to the NCO and directed his observations to a causeway and Bailey bridge across cratered and flooded ground less than two miles ahead.

"Looks like they're stuck." Adjusting the setting to suit his weaker sight, Hyde scrutinized the distant tableau.

Four figures stood about a Rangerover that had stopped on the log built causeway leading to the bridge, a little short of a section that had partially subsided into the artificially created bog.

"Do we go in on foot and grab them now, or wait for the track to be fixed?" Hyde returned the glasses.

"I think we'll wait for the wagon." Something else caught Revell's attention. "In fact we'll have to."

Midway between them and their quarry he'd seen a pair of light trucks and a field car parked among the trees, far enough in for them to have been invisible from the road. In the course of the day they'd seen dozens of rusting wrecks and at first glance that was all those three vehicles had registered as, but then instinct made him focus on them again, and a more critical inspection revealed that they weren't hulks.

It was the trucks' erected canvas tilts that betrayed them. Tough though the material was, it would not have survived several months' continual exposure to Europe's unrelenting elements. If they'd been derelicts then there ought only to have been a few flapping strips by this time, but that wasn't how it was.

The transports were all late models that, aside from

being mud spattered, appeared to be in perfect condition. That discovery made, it didn't take Revell long to discover what they were doing there.

Scrutinizing every yard of ground between the vehicles and the highway he found their passengers dug-in and occupying hastily camouflaged positions astride it.

With the advantage of height, Revell could discern the textbook precision with which the slit trenches and weapons pits were laid out.

"There's the best part of a platoon of Russian infantry waiting for us. Seems like we'll have to run the gauntlet of whatever they've got to throw before we'll reach those turncoat civies."

"And it doesn't look like they're prepared to hang about and wait for us either." Even without the binoculars Hyde could tell from the patterns of movement about the Rangerover that efforts were being made to repair the causeway.

"Okay, the schedule's too tight for us to play Indians and sneak up behind that ambush . . ."

"Not much chance of that anyway, with the racket the Marder makes."

"Right." Revell had already recognized that impediment to any attempt at stealth. "So we'll just have to get as close as we can before they open fire. If we charge in with cannon blazing they'll hit us with a shower of anti-tank rockets. The road's not that wide, and there's nowhere else to go, so . . ."

"So . . . ?" Not that he needed to ask, Hyde was perfectly able to anticipate what was coming next.

"And so we motor toward them like we're on a Sunday afternoon drive round the park, make out we don't even know they're there. You know what the Ruskies are like. Offer them a sitting target and they'll wait until they're within spitting distance before letting them have it. A second or two before they have a go at us, we'll pour all we've got into them."

"Sounds fine in theory, Major. Do you think we can make the timing that neat?"

"Look, it's all we've got. Let's get ready to put it into practice."

Walking back to the Marder, a thought kept nagging at Hyde. While they were still out of hearing of the rest of the squad he posed the officer a question whose answer he suspected he already knew. "If we had all the time in the world, Major, you'd still have us doing it this way, wouldn't you."

"What's the matter, sergeant, you think you can live forever?"

"Just a day at a time, but if I've got to cop it then I don't want to go knowing that I've taken some of my men with me who didn't have to die. Most of the blokes I've met in the Zone want to win the war by surviving it, not by throwing their lives away."

Revell could pretend, to himself at least, that their proximity to the rest of the squad precluded him from making a suitable reply. In all truth he couldn't argue with the NCO, the sergeant was right; it was he who was wrong. Not that he could stop himself though. It was as if he was trying to make all the war he could, trying to keep the biggest possible share for himself.

In some such actions might have been a death wish, but he didn't recognize that within him. And even if that were the case then long before now he'd have had it granted. The Zone would have found it all too easy to fulfill. It did as much for thousands of others every day, when death was the last thing they desired.

Unbidden, unwanted, to the forefront of his mind came a recollection of the pathetic group they'd provided with an escape from the Zone. Even in their case though there had been no willingness to embrace death in the solution they'd found to their suffering, distressing in the extreme though it was.

When they'd set out to cross the Zone to reach the west those people had been full of hope. To have got so far that hope must have stayed with them until their condition had deteriorated beyond the point of endurance. They hadn't wanted to die, and nor did he, but as he climbed back into the Marder, Revell knew that, like them, for him there was no longer a choice.

CHAPTER EIGHT

"Really, I'm not at all sure that this is entirely practical. I wait to be convinced." With his free hand keeping a fierce grip on the Rover's tailgate mounted spare wheel, Edwards made feeble attempts to cut the rope lashing rough-trimmed logs together. "You do realize that once we have removed these from behind us we shall be quite cut off, should the repair to the track ahead not be successful." He looked at the ochre water beneath the piling suspended causeway. "I should not like to have to wade back to firm ground."

"Give it a rest, will you." Sherry took the axe from the professor and with a single double handed blow freed the timber for Gross to lift. "Go up front and help Webb place and tie the logs we bring you."

As the nervous academic edged past the high sided vehicle, Gross leered at the woman. "Did you get rid of him so it'd be just you and me?"

"Oh yeah." She started on another binding, the blunt blade taking several hacks to get through the plaited strands. "Oh yeah, all day I been saying to myself how much I'd love to have your smelly fat gut crushing my bare arse into splintered wood while your soft little prick had trouble finding its dribbling way through my fanny hair."

"I like it when you talk dirty, makes my balls go tight." Half closing his eyes Gross puckered his wet lips toward her.

"In a minute I'll make you leak something, you creep." Raising her axe threateningly, Sherry took a half pace back to make room to swing it. As she did her ankle turned, and she lost her balance.

With surprising speed for his bulk Gross grabbed her, and then as he pulled back, crushed her to him while his hips thrust the hard tip of his penis against the front seam of her jeans.

"See, it's not a soft little prick, is it. I reckon it'd even fill that well used cavern of a cunt you've got. Want to talk dirty again? Go on, I could jerk off with one hand just listening to you."

Managing to break free she pulled her T-shirt straight where Gross had tried to shove his hand inside it. "Jesus, have you ever taken a look at yourself? You're horrible."

Undecided whether or not to grab for her again, Gross stood panting, watching her breasts heave as she also fought for breath. "What are you getting so fussy about. I've seen all your films, all of them, even those early shorts. My favorite was that one called The Boarding School, especially that scene where the caretaker and the boilerman hoisted your gymslip and had you front and back among the cobwebs in the cellar. Were they really buggering and fucking you at the same time? Did they shove their tools right in? Or was that imitation spunk they licked off you afterwards?"

"Someone should shove something up you, a loaded scattergun maybe." There was more Sherry would have said, but from the front of the Rover Webb was calling for another log. Keeping a wary eye on Gross, she resumed work.

Places of weather-stained rope, strips of peeling bark and chips of wood made a continual rain into the tainted water a couple of feet below the level of the causeway. The same evil smelling solution colored the contents of all the other bomb-made pits carpeting the land.

Beyond the elevated track and the girder bridge that took the route finally to firm ground once more, the landscape took on a curiously monochrome appearance.

Trees and grass, every living thing, or everything that had been living because there was no sign of life to be seen in any blade or leaf, everything seemed to have been literally leached of all color. The countryside had been turned gray, the trunks and boughs of trees dark, their foliage a paler shade, but all of them gray. It was as if that part of the world had been dusted with an adhering ash that no deluge could remove.

A few wind-blown leaves scrunched beneath their feet, crackling apart like a fine brittle china. Some of the fragments fell between the logs to float on the sickly yellow water, skimming back and forth at the whim of the lightest air current.

Struggling to wedge a final component of the

temporary repair into place, Webb ceased work abruptly as he heard a fusillade of cannon and automatic fire from behind them.

"How close is that? Could it have to do with us?" Becoming agitated Edwards opened a door and prepared to climb into the back of the Rangerover.

"I don't know. A mile or so, perhaps, but it's definitely on the road we've travelled." Resorting to stamping on it, without success, Webb had to content himself with leaving the oversized length of wood projecting above the others about it.

"Then why are we waiting." Setting an example of urgency he hoped the others would follow, Edwards reached for a hand-hold to haul himself in, missed it, and lost his footing on the high step. Teetering, he gave a high pitched yelp of alarm, then with arms flailing fell backward into the polluted water half filling a large crater.

Not eighteen inches deep, he floundered and panicked as if thrown into the deep end. "Oh, help me, help me someone, get me out, oh it's revolting, I'm wet . . ."

Extending the handle of the axe for him to grip, Sherry and Webb assisted the professor back to the causeway. He sat gasping and spluttering.

A belly laugh from Gross at his mud-smeared and bedraggled condition did nothing to soothe Edwards' ruffled dignity and composure, but it did stimulate the speed of his recovery from the shock of his unexpected immersion. "Be quiet you uncouth braying fool. Oh damn, damn, damn. I'm quite soaked through. Get me a blanket someone, quickly.

While Edwards installed himself in a corner of the

rear seat, and Gross tried and failed to grope Sherry as he assisted her into the front passenger seat, Webb unlashed a petrol can from the roof rack and began to splash its contents over the causeway behind them.

The empty container he tossed aside, to slowly settle in the same miniature lake that had so recently accommodated Edwards. When he bent down and flicked his lighter at the periphery of the soaked area he had to recoil swiftly as the spilt fuel ignited with a roar.

Black smoke billowed from the breeze-feathered tops of the licking flame, as liquid fire dripped off the logs to spread across the ground below.

Hurrying back to the driver's seat he started the engine, and with a glance through his rear view mirror at the boiling smoke, eased the Rangerover forward onto the improvised repair they had effected.

Lurching from side to side, from beneath the four wheel drive vehicle came a chorus of creaking protest from imperfectly positioned timbers. There was a sharp crack as one snapped, the sudden loud twang of a rope binding parting, but momentum was maintained and wallowing dramatically the Rover dragged itself across the disintegrating section and onto the Bailey bridge that comprised the final link with the far side.

Webb's last sight of the causeway revealed it to be a blazing wreck on the verge of total collapse. Fire raged along it, spreading even as he looked and shreds of burning rope and bark made a non-stop shower into the water. He would have enjoyed seeing its collapse, it would have marked their final separation from the west, underlined and reinforced their commitment to the east. Eventually it would fall, even though he would not see it, and that knowledge was satisfaction enough.

"You can relax, the worst is over. Whatever it was that was happening behind us, we cannot be caught now. From this moment we can enjoy a gentle drive to our destination and a pleasant reception."

Professor Edwards heard but paid no attention. Through the discomfort of being wet and cold he could feel something else; a prickling, mildly burning sensation. Alternately he scratched or applied pressure to those parts of his body where the sensation was becoming most acute. It seemed mostly confined to the lower half of his person, those parts that had been immersed, but he could sense it also where the filthy water had splashed on his face and hands.

Trying to be discreet, and decent about it, he fumbled beneath the blanket and hoisted the leg of his trousers. The skin had an unhealthy blanched look and was crisscrossed by red marks that revealed where creases in his damp clothes had been in closest contact with his leg.

The growing discomfort of the irritating affliction forced him to pluck at his clothes to prevent even that light contact, but that was not enough, the burning and itching was becoming worse, unendurable.

Casting all thought of propriety aside with the blanket he took the only course open. Tortured by intolerable discomfort that was fast transforming into pain he mewed his distress as he took recourse to the only measure the torment prompted in his distracted mind.

"Holy Jesus." Hearing the commotion Sherry

110

turned to look. "Has the old guy gone off his trolley?"

Edwards had managed to strip to his woolen underpants when he finally lost control and howled as he went berserk.

Automatic fire of every caliber spat from the Marder on Revell's order. Cannon shells and machine gun tracer slashed through the trees at the roadside. Timed to perfection, the onslaught hit the Russian ambush an instant before it was to be sprung.

From the turret Ripper kept hosing shells from the slim barrel of the Rheinmetal cannon. His targets were invisible, but experience had taught him the hard way from what sort of position and angle to expect concealed enemy fire. Every possible location he saturated with a storm of armor-piercing and explosive shot.

Not once did he see the men he was firing at, but there were moments when he could tell he was firing with effect. Sometimes it was a gout of bright light as his rounds ignited a Russian's smoke grenades, or a fountain of white fire as he set off spare machine gun magazines in a weapon pit.

From the steady cruising speed with which they'd approached the Russian ambush, Burke pushed the mileage-worn engine to its limit and beyond. But even so, as they surged ahead streams of bullets hit the hull's angled armor, beating a hail on the metal as they deformed against it or bounced off.

A hastily aimed anti-tank rocket soared from a clump of saplings and skimmed over the steeply raked bow plate as an uncomfortably near miss. Another blasted the road a few yards in front of their threshing tracks and sent fragments smashing into the APC's frontal armor. The largest pieces, travelling at incredible velocity, actually dented the hardened plate. Smaller chunks of the bomb's casing, and lumps of asphalt starred but failed to penetrate observation prisms in the command cupola.

Grenades exploded on the hull top. Ripper felt their concussion through the extra thick protection of the turret walls, but instinct told him they were almost past the worst. There were few targets to the front or side, only the rear facing remotely controlled machine gun remained in constant action. It was tempting to traverse the turret, to join in the engagement of those communist troops who made the mistake of thinking they could run from hiding into the center of the road and fire at the carrier's more vulnerable vertical rear armor, but a warning from Revell kept him watching the road ahead for a Russian backstop position.

Tearing around a bend they drove straight into it. A poorly camouflaged Soviet field car was beneath trees at the roadside. Resisting the near overwhelming urge to destroy the soft-skin target presented to him at point-blank range, Ripper traversed the cannon in search of the vehicle's occupants. They found him first.

"Top of the embankment on your right . . ."

Already elevating the weapon as fast as he could, as he heard the major's shouted warning he had to instinctively duck as a machine gun splashed blindingly bright tracer across his periscopes and sight.

Retaliation had to wait while he blinked his vision clear, and regaining it, the first thing he saw was a flame-tailed rocket coming straight at him.

Opening fire, he knew it was already too late. In the couple of seconds before impact, as he watched his shells blasting bodies apart on the embankment, through his mind raced a flickering selection of terrifying images. Dominant among them was that of their sergeant's fire-ravaged features. Ripper saw it superimposed on his own, as the warhead of the same type that had burned away Hyde's facial tissue and reduced him to a wicked parody of human appearance, closed range.

Striking the turret front, the rocket's lethal payload detonated instantaneously and focused into a pencil thin jet of pure energy, bored into the armor.

The air in the turret became roasting hot and was filled with smoke and stinging bright sparks and the smell of furnace heated metal.

"Jesus, I'm on fire, I'm on fire." Thrashing about to reach the area of searing pain, Ripper slipped from his seat and fell to the cabin floor. He felt wads of cloth and packs being bundled against him to smother the flames, then tasted a mouthful of the bitter contents of a gushing fire-extinguisher.

"Leave him, use it on the turret. The fire suppression system isn't working." Grabbing and hauling clear the smoke-blinded gunner, Revell unhooked another pyrene and aimed its billowing discharge upward, toward the glow at the center of the dense smoke filling the turret and command cupola.

"Am I burned? I got to know, tell me. How's my face?" There was no reply to Ripper's frantic plea. He tried to get a hold of a leg to detain someone, any one of those who constantly trampled him, but his attempts were kicked or stamped aside, and he could only listen to the noises as the crew fought to contain the blaze.

In the absence of any order to the contrary, Burke kept the APC going flat out. He'd seen too many other squads die when they'd bailed out prematurely, still within small arms range of the enemy, when they could have stayed with their transport longer, ridden it safely into cover. Repeatedly he smashed his fist down on the button that should have manually countered any malfunction in the automatic extinguishers, but the square of green plastic set in the control panel, that would have signalled its activation, remained stubbornly unlit.

"Clear the way." With shoulder and elbow Thorne pushed the others aside as he pulled the flamethrower cylinders from beneath the dribble of molten plastic and metal and shifted them to comparative safety behind the driver's seat.

"Are you fucking mad?" A glance as they bumped the seat-back told Burke what it was that had been moved to share his portion of the interior. "Move those blasted things away from me, stuff them through a bloody hatch."

"At a pinch any of us could handle this crate, but you can't spit fire, so you go through the hatch. We need this more than you." Thorne leaned forward so that their driver got the full benefit of his broad smile.

"We've got it licked." Revell's throat felt like it was lined with a coarse grained sandpaper. His extin-

114

guisher was almost empty, but the yellow glow of the fire was gone. "Cut in the air conditioning again. We'll motor another mile or so to be on the safe side, then stop for a check of what systems are still functioning."

"The stop'll have to be now. Fancy a spot more fire-fighting?" Bringing the APC to rest on the gentle incline of a compacted stone ramp up to the causeway, Burke looked along the length of the wooden structure.

A hundred yards of its center, unnaturally dried by the harsh chemicals with which it had been saturated, impregnated with the oil dripped from thousands of sumps and back axles, was blazing. It was a great roaring avenue of flame.

CHAPTER NINE

". . . but our troops do report several hits, Comrade Colonel." Alternately sweating and shivering with nervous tension, the major steeled himself for an answering blast as violent as those that had greeted the rest of his report.

Rozenkov considered himself something of an artist, a master even, when it came to instilling terror. Like any other art, the inflicting of fear could not be played all on one note, or portrayed all in one color: contrasts were called for, and he used one now. He lowered his voice until it was almost a whisper, purging it of any overtones of menace, replacing it with gentle amusement.

"Oh, that is most interesting, then I take it that the NATO squad still in pursuit of the delegation are ghosts."

There was a trap here, the liaison officer could sense it, but there was no escape to be found, he had to reply. "It would appear, Comrade Colonel, that the hits failed to penetrate their armor . . ."

"Even more interesting. Perhaps you would care to inform me what caliber of weapons are issued to your troops, what type of ammunition. I am sure also that if they are using standard issue equipment our armament experts will be intrigued to discover what level of incompetence is required to render ineffective their tried and tested inventions."

Again the major knew an answer was called for, was expected, but he had none. Anticipating the colonel's next words to be the ordering of his arrest, those that came were all the greater surprise.

"Never mind, Major Morkov. The results of the GRU's abortive attempt to halt the pursuit, no better than I expected, will have had the precise effect on the civilians that I required. They will have heard the engagement, perhaps even guessed its significance, but whether they have or not they will now know that there is only one way they can go, eastward, straight into our waiting arms."

"I understand, Comrade Colonel. We will use the NATO squad to drive them on."

"You do not begin to understand." Rozenkov shoved a bulky file across the desk. "It has cost the KGB a well planted agent of influence and two senior field operatives to discover the composition of that pursuit group. We have brushed with them before, perhaps military intelligence has also. See for yourself."

The fat folder was well thumbed, greasy and torn where it had been often and carelessly handled, its cover marked by overlapping coffee rings. "I have heard of this Special Combat Group, Comrade Colonel, but I have not personally had occasion . . ."

Lips curling in a sneering smile, Rozenkov enjoyed the KGB's moment of superiority over Military Intelligence. He gathered the file back to him, clumsily patting straight the edges of the stack of paper and only succeeding in adding more creases to the unaligned sheets.

"They are a miniature private army, a rag-bag assortment of mercenaries and deserters from several countries armed forces, led by an American major. We knew they were in disfavor, thought they had been disbanded, but they have turned up again."

"Surely, they cannot number more than a dozen, they can pose no threat?"

"In the past they have been more than a threat. Several important operations have been spoiled by them. There are officers above us both who would be higher still had it not been for the activities of that squad. Today they have, for once, served not hindered our purpose. It would be fitting if that were their last act. The next time let there be no mistake. Wipe them from existence and we shall both do ourselves some good. Fail, and I shall make certain that any blame attaches to you."

Behind the desk a large scale map of Bavaria had been tacked to the wall. A pink headed pin marked the approximate position of the civilians, a sparse scattering of blues represented the GRU units racing to intercept their pursuers. There were two more pins, both a luminous red. They were at present stuck in the plaster just off the edge of the map.

Those were the KGB spetsnaz units being hastily briefed for the reception. Once they were on the map it would not be for them the same slow overland progress as the Military Intelligence companies. Aboard fast helicopter gunships available to such elite units they would race in, covering at speed difficult territory that others were crossing at a comparative crawl.

The major recalled his commanding officer's parting instructions before he'd transferred to this liaison post with the KGB. He was to trust no one, confide in no one, and bide his time, wait for the big opportunity. In the fierce perpetual competition between the State Security Force and Military Intelligence, more than simple prestige hung on the outcome of the more important operations.

Whatever the result of this one in particular, he knew he could expect no favors from Rozenkov, no credit for success, no protection in failure. Win or lose, the operation's conclusion would only mark the onset of more doubt and danger for him. On the other hand, if he played a double game, performing his liaison tasks adequately while setting thing so that the GRU could step in and take the credit, then his stock would ride high with his own commander and he would be whisked away to a more attractive post, beyond Colonel Rozenkov's malevolent gaze and reach.

He would set to work at once, but he would have to tread carefully. "Is that all, Comrade Colonel?"

Dismissing the officer with a grunt and a wave of his hand, Rozenkov continued his scrutiny of the map, hardly noticing the quiet click of the door catch as it was gently pulled shut.

In a mind trained to watch for detail, for any betraying gesture or intonation, the near imperceptible change in the usual manner in which the major left the room registered with his intrigue-honed thought processes, and for a second he gave it consideration.

There was a brief overlap as he referred his concentration back to the map. A mental card index went to file the thought away, but the instant before it was filed from sight an unlooked for cross-reference was made.

The colonel let his eyes stray from the center of the map to the pair of red-topped pins not yet in use, and then back to the sprinkling of yellow. He looked at them for a long time.

"Shitty great fuss to make over a couple of little holes." Dooley watched as Ripper's burns were attended to.

Andrea dusted an antiseptic into the deep dark-ringed pits in the young American's shoulder where the molten metal had splashed on him, then taped a field dressing over them. "You can let him go."

"I could do with a cigarette." Ripper flexed his wrists after Dooley released his powerful grip. "Can somebody pass me mine, it'll take a minute for me to get any feeling back into my fingers. This great ape had cut off my circulation." Hell, he needed a smoke. The worst bit had been when the girl had cut away his scorched NBC smock. Charred pieces of the thick cloth had fastened to his flesh. In the more lightly burned areas outside the confines of the sterile bandage he could see the pattern of the material's weave.

Delving into a smoldering, blackened pack, Clarence produced a small handful of gray ash. "Rather looks as if your special handrolls have gone up in smoke." He let the light powder run through his fingers to dust the floor.

"Then he'll just have to stay in the real world with the rest of us." Hyde came down from the turret. "And his first brush with cruel reality is to find out that he's back in the infantry. The cannon is buggered good and proper, so's the co-axial mount and the last of the smoke discharges. I want a couple of volunteers to heave the twenty-millimeter ammo out. From here on it's just excess baggage." Two of the squad were a little slow in avoiding his eyes. "You'll do nicely, get to it."

As Thorne and Dooley set about searching every rack, locker and ammunition box, the Marder began to splash through the acres of shallow flooding on the periphery of the heavily cratered area.

Coiled and snaking belts of mixed cannon shells began to mark their route.

Altogether the detour took them three miles out of their way, but with the terrain involved only marginally better than that they were seeking a way around, it cost them ninety precious minutes.

Estimates Revell made as to how long it would be

before they rejoined the road again, and were once more on the Rangerover's trail, had constantly to be revised as their driver was able for a while to increase speed on a patch of more favorable going and then had to slow to a crawl to negotiate or find a way to avoid giant craters that loomed suddenly before them, partially hidden by a sickly yellow drifting mist that was rising from the sulphurous ground.

Gathering darkness was also taking a hand in concealing the ugly countryside, but the sinking blood-red sun was playing a last few tricks with the light, turning the dull gray foliage of the distant trees a delicate pale pink, and tinting the mist with an orange glow.

"Doesn't look like we're on earth at all, does it." In the fast fading light it was difficult for Burke to decide whether to use his naked eye or switch to infrared or white light illumination. He settled for a compromise, using an image intensifying prism that he pulled like a visor over his vision port.

As they drove onto solid ground, and the Marder nosed into the trees, it rapidly became obvious that the image intensifier alone would be insufficient. With that single drab shade predominating there were hardly any reference points. Tree trunks, bushes, the very grass, they all merged into one.

After narrowly missing a third collision with elms that had materialized from the uniform backdrop when only yards off, Burke decided to use the shielded headlamps, choosing to employ white light.

Only the left hand beam came on, and that was weakened by a thick coating of mud. A further substantial portion of its usefulness was cancelled by its being reflected back by thickening streamers of ground fog tailing into the woods.

"Give the Ruskies another year and they'll have the whole bloody world in this state, if they're not stopped." Heaving clear the last of the cannon shells, Thorne secured the hatch before retrieving his flame-thrower and commencing a thorough check of its every component.

"Shit, what'd be the point of that." At their slow pace through the trees, with the engine revs kept low, Dooley discovered that he didn't have to shout at the top of his voice to be heard. "What good's it gonna do them if they win the war and what they capture ain't fit for nothing. Fuck it, that don't make any sort of sense."

"It is not always possible to reason, to think, the way a communist would." Taking advantage of the gentler ride Boris was repairing electronic circuits damaged by the direct hit. "When they cannot get what they want they would rather destroy it than let others have its use."

Boris was thinking back to his time in Moscow, to the moment when he had started to admit to himself how conditions really were in Russia. Until then he had kept his head down, like every one else, got on with his life and either pretended not to see or made excuses for what even his deliberate self-blinkering could not fail to notice.

It was those ten days at the Stalinskachowskii military prison in the city that had finally forced him to open his eyes. Those two hundred and forty hours had seemed more like that many million. There, in the name of the State and Party, carried out by members of the KGB and GRU he had witnessed greater cruelty and depravity than until then he'd known existed.

Prisoners had been forced to eat their own excreta, the young ones had been buggered by relays of brutish guards until they bled and had to be stitched without anesthetics. And there was the petty, vicious, mind breaking vindictiveness of the constant roll calls and searches and punishments . . .

Ten days he had been given for the wine stain on his dress uniform. Within a day of arriving he'd had a further forty added for offenses so trivial he'd found it hard to believe them when they'd been read aloud in the chief warder's office. He hadn't laughed, not even let his face twitch but as if they could read his mind and to punish him for what was in it, he was kicked all the way back to his cell and then beaten for an hour by warders who left no part of his body untouched.

Only a special order clearing the prison of men fit for the front had saved his sanity and very likely his life. Like most of the rest of the draft he'd had to crawl to the trucks and as they'd been driven away he had heard the screams of the men left behind, begging to be allowed to join the fighting. With those pleas and screams had been the laughter of the guards as they trooped back inside to quell the noise from the cripples in their own sadistic fashion.

Complaining loudly, Ripper surrendered the length of bench on which he'd been reclining, and sat up.

"You lot, you just ain't got no feelings for the sick."

"You're fit enough. Get into a fresh suit, that one's in bloody ribbons."

"Hey, come on Sarge, you're kidding me, ain't you. Since when have I been a bendy toy. I'm wounded, see? How am I going to struggle into an NBC outfit."

"All that's wrong with you is a few minor burns. You'd have worse if I'd stubbed a couple of cigars on your scrawny carcass." Hyde was about to let it go at that, but he had an idea to speed the American's change. "But then maybe I'm being unfair. How about if I get one of the others to help you, someone with a delicate and caring touch, maybe Dooley . . ."

"Sarge, you just don't appreciate my condition. I could do with the help, but not Dooley. He ain't learned to dress himself proper yet. I'd end up crammed into a sleeve with my head poking out the cuff."

"How about Andrea then," moving aside Hyde let her pass.

"I will not hurt you, much . . ."

Ripper yelled at her approach and clutched together the gaping front of his NBC suit as Andrea went to slit it open with a razor honed bayonet. "I ain't about to let no woman near my vitals with a blade. Get her away from me."

"That's enough." Hearing the commotion Revell ducked down from the command cupola. "Quit the games and get back to your positions. Ripper, you get a fresh suit on without help. If you'd been watching the chemical level indicator you'd have noticed that the contamination reading is going off the scale under these trees. If the air conditioning fails we'll only have a minute or so before this much starts to find a way in."

Nothing more was needed to prompt Ripper and he found the sudden use of his bandaged arm and shoulder as he started to shed the torn garment.

Slowly and very deliberately Andrea sheathed the bayonet, letting the back of her hand brush against Thorne. Her eyes met the major's, and held them for a long moment.

Resentment and jealousy difficult to suppress near overwhelmed Revell's self-control when he saw their fingers briefly touched. The contact looked accidental, but he was well aware that there was very little Andrea ever did by accident. Searching for a pretext to part them, he told Andrea to bring the map board to the radio console. Pushing Boris from his place, he accepted the board and then pretended preoccupation with marking their precise location.

Provocatively Andrea leaned over his shoulder to examine the map. He could feel her firm right breast against his back, and immediately sensed the acute discomfort of an erection suddenly stiffening when he could not put his hand down to arrange its more comfortable accommodation among the tight folds of his pants.

She didn't wear any perfume, but she still managed to smell feminine. In an utterly shapeless NBC suit, the curves of her body further hidden by the grenades and other weaponry festooning it, she exuded sexuality. Her breath was on his neck and cheek as she bent closer to speak.

"There is something I want from you."

They were the words he'd have given anything to hear, but despite the leaping sensation in his chest he said nothing, waiting for her to go on.

"After we have caught those civilians, those traitors, there is something I want you to do. It is some thing . . . special."

He didn't dare to speculate, to hope what her next words would be. Was this a sign that she had chosen him in preference to Hyde? The pause became agonizingly long, and his impatience grew with it. "Well? What is it, what do you want me to do?" Damn it! He'd have done anything, couldn't think of a single thing he'd have refused her.

"After we catch them, when we have them safe, I want you to give them to me."

Disappointment, bitter anger and frustration surged through him. Fighting to control the rage that whirled and merged with the overpowering emotions bottled inside of him, he didn't feel the marker pen clenched in his tightening fist deform and burst to stain his palm red.

"Why do you want them, so you can get in some practice killing civilians?"

"You should know that I hardly need that, Major. Have you forgotten Hamburg so soon?"

Revell felt his mind being crushed by her words as though each were another massive weight loading a press. There was a question that begged to be asked, but he couldn't bring himself to utter it. Instead he tried to read an answer from her beautiful face but it had set hard and was as devoid of expression as

Sergeant Hyde's. With nothing to be learned that way, the question rose through the many layers of repression that tried ineffectually to smother it and emerged in a hesitant stutter.

"I remember . . . Hamburg. You were wounded . . . noncombatant . . . you worked with a radio location unit in the city . . . took no part in the fighting . . . When . . . when would you have had the chance?"

"On the last day, when the garrison broke through the Russian cordon, many of their agents in the city were desperate to get out. They became careless, broadcast for too long. We heard them pleading for instructions, and we found them. Did you know that your friend, Inga, was an agent?"

All Revell could do was give an almost imperceptible shake of his head. It was not the whole truth, but the words that would have qualified his denial would also have choked him.

"We had a long talk. About you."

Now Revell could see a trace of expression in her face, a subtle alteration of the line of her lips, a slight widening of the eyes. It was a rare blend of amusement and cruelty, of contempt and self-assurance.

"Surely you are interested in what we discussed?" Leaning forward a fraction more so that her mouth was by his ear, Andrea feigned absorption with the map. "She told me everything, everything that you did together, or perhaps I should say what she had you do to her. I think she was well pleased, especially when you used your tongue. She said you made her very wet, so wet that you were almost sick when it

129

filled your mouth. But you didn't stop, did you? You did as you were told, as she ordered."

The words came whisper soft, so faintly that they were on the threshold of his hearing, but to Revell it seemed that each was screamed so loud that all the crew must hear. He would have made her stop, somehow, anyhow, but was hypnotized by her voice and the memories it brought back.

"And also I had her show me how you kissed. She did it well."

"You're lying, you've got to be lying." Revell hissed the combined accusation and denial and though audible only to Andrea it was more filled with feeling than yelling it at the top of his voice would have conveyed.

"Perhaps you would like to believe that, but I know that you do not. Do you recall the taste of her lipstick, of her mouth? I do, it was sweet, like tasting a perfume."

"Where, when did you talk to her?" There was a sickening frightened feeling welling inside him. He had to know, and she was going to tell him anyway. Better that it came quick so that he start to learn to live with it, if he could.

"It was at her apartment, at about the time you were leading the attack on the Russian trenches, I should think. You had done so much together . . . for her . . . that it took a long time to tell, and to show me."

"And what do you intend doing with the information you share?"

"Oh, I am sure I can find a use for what I know,

but you are wrong about my sharing the knowledge with Inga, Major Revell. I never share, not anything. Before I left the apartment I made sure that there was no one to share it with."

CHAPTER TEN

"For fuck's sake, can't you keep him quiet?" Unable to tolerate the howling any longer, Gross left the room and went out into the overgrown beer garden. Shit, he'd had enough. If it'd be up to him he'd have turned the Rangerover about and headed back, except that there was a good reason why they couldn't. They'd literally burned their bridges behind them.

Not bothering to find a place out of view of the window he opened his pants and emptied his bladder on to the de-foliant withered stems of lupines. In the hope that the woman would look out and see him he took his time over tucking his penis away, shaking it thoroughly and playing with its circumcised head between his pudgy fingers before reluctantly conceding that she was not going to be so obliging.

If that autocratic prig Webb hadn't been with them he'd have screwed her by now, opened those plump thighs of hers and given her the full benefit. He could almost imagine it. Best if she was sprawled back over a table, legs wide apart and dangling, so that he could see his penetration over the rim of his paunch.

It'd be lovely to hear her shout of protest as he withdrew at the moment of coming and shot the full load, in jerking spurts over her belly and into her fanny hair.

He'd pull her hand through it, to show her how much he'd done, then have her rub it all over her fat udders. Sweat coursed down him at the thought. Moving back toward the inn, he stopped where he could see her clearly and undid his pants again. Already blood-pumped to rock hardness, with practiced single hand strokes he began to masturbate.

At the third, and most prolonged, application of the cleaning-fluid soaked rag over his mouth and nose, Professor Edwards finally gave up the struggle, and after gagging violently, lapsed into unconsciousness. Even then his head continued to loll from side to side and his clumsily bandaged hands made involuntary jerking movements toward those parts of his torso most thickly covered by the big mounds of yellow blisters.

"That is all I can do for him." Webb threw the rag aside, then had second thoughts and retrieved it, stowing it in a pack with the dusty half-empty plastic bottle from which the makeshift anesthetic had come, on top of the small metal-boxed medical kit that had proved so pathetically inadequate. "If I eke it out, and we make good time the rest of the way then he can be kept like that. The Russians will be able to treat him."

"He looks horrible. What is it?" All of her will power had been needed to prevent Sherry vomiting when she'd first seen the old man's condition.

His emaciated body would not have been a pretty sight at any time, his anemic flesh sagging in flaccid wrinkles, his withered genitals bracketed by the distended mounds of a double hernia. With much of it covered and discolored by huge raised blisters that made it even less attractive.

"There must have been a chemical in the water, a modern derivation of mustard gas perhaps. What ever it was it was present in sufficient strength to do what you see here. If he'd swallowed any quantity of it he'd be dead by now, but I don't think he has, although a little of it does seem to have splashed on his face."

Sherry couldn't bring herself to step close enough to see where Webb was indicating. From her youngest days, from as far back as she could remember, right from when her mother had enrolled her with the child model agency, virtually every moment of her life had been in some way concerned with her appearance. Cosmetics, clothes, her hair, how she walked, smiled, talked, how she smelled: every waking moment filled with such things and thoughts of them, and most of the people around her had been similarly occupied with themselves.

A greater contrast with that narcistic world than the Zone could not have been found. Any blemish, any deformed or ugly thing she found utterly distasteful and avoided, or had avoided. Here she was being presented with the incarnation of all that she most abhorred; gross disfigurement, old age, sickness,

135

suffering . . .

"Feeling faint?" Still beaded with perspiration from the effort of attaining his orgasm, Gross entered the room, pausing to wipe his sticky fingers on faded curtains that gave off clouds of dust. "You need a drink. This should be just the place to find some. This way I think . . ."

"We should only consume such supplies as we brought with us." Calling after the fat man, Webb's words trailed off as Gross went down the cellar steps.

"Don't be such a fucking old woman."

His reply to the caution came back to them amid the clinking of bottles, and was followed by a loud crash in turn succeeded by the prolonged sound of breaking glass.

"Shit, it's as black as fucking hell down there. Get me a torch from the . . . no, don't bother, I've found a candle."

A minute later he reappeared at the top of the stairs, his arms laden with bottles, and more protruding from the baggy pockets of his sports jacket.

"Really, I'm quite serious, you shouldn't even consider drinking any of those . . ." Webb declined the slim necked green bottle thrust at him. ". . . they could be contaminated."

"Oh piss off, you fucking kill-joy." Depositing his load on a table, not bothering to catch a Reisling that rolled off to shatter on the stone floor, he delved through the interior of the medical kit until he discovered a small bottle of antiseptic.

Choosing a sparkling white completely at random, he liberally splashed a third of the disinfectant over the gold foil wrapped about the wine's wire bound cork, wiping the surplus off immediately on his sleeve.

"There, that'll do it, you fussy sod. Here, try a bit." The cork came free with a bang as he wrenched at it, and a spout of foam splattered the floor and his shoes.

Again Webb declined, instead going over to Edwards to wrap a blanket about him. "We should keep moving. There is still a good distance to travel."

"So what's your hurry. If there was someone after us, there's not now, not with that bridge down. Isn't that right, my little aging starlet?"

Sherry Kane also refused the offer of a drink, but immediately wished she'd accepted the offered bottle, just so as she could hit him with it. Gross made her shudder, he was so repulsive. There had been times, when she was resting, and the rent was due, when she'd had to take Johns like that . . . like the slob in the green Chevrolet with the stickers in the windows. He'd wanted her to piss on him. When his offer had reached a hundred she'd done it, standing astride him as he lay in the filth of a service road behind Sunset Boulevard.

Afterward she'd had to shower a dozen times. Not that he'd touched her, just laid there shining that pencil torch beam up her miniskirt and making gurgling noises like a baby. She'd been busting to go anyway, but it had taken a good ten minutes . . .

Gross reminded her of that one. In fact he reminded her of all the bad ones, all rolled together; the orals when they wouldn't use a sheath and forced her to swallow, the anals who wanted it rough and wouldn't use cream, the fanny hair pluckers, the

137

biters . . .

Getting no response, no acceptance of his invitation to imbibe with him, Gross contented himself with sitting on a railback chair and making suggestive motions toward the woman by circling his fingers about the neck of the bottle and running them up and down.

He drank fast, belching loudly after every other pull. "Not bad this stuff. Don't usually drink much plonk myself, leave it to French peasants and the trendy wine bar crowd, unless it's free that is, at some buckshee union do." He threw his head back to drain the last drops, then chose another from the selection before him. After an even more cursory decontamination than he'd carried out on the first, he opened and started into a hock.

"Those stuck up gits I had to negotiate with probably drank this stuff, you know, the pin striped, poe faced captains of British industry. I killed one of them you know, really." Tapping the side of his wide-pored bulbous nose he winked at Sherry. "You don't believe me do you, either of you?"

"Believe what?" Beginning to lose his patience, Webb was provoked into the snap. It defeated its own purpose, not silencing the union boss, but giving him encouragement.

"That I killed a shitty white collar crud. Well I did, with this." He stuck out his furred tongue and wagged it from side to side.

A glimpse was enough for Webb, and he busied himself with lighting ornamental candles set in wall fittings, as the last of the evening's light faded.

"Nine hours the dumb fucker was sat opposite me.

138

Every time he increased the offer, I upped the demands. When he said he'd introduce a bonus scheme I said the brothers didn't want one, when he withdrew it I said we wanted it. He had to settle on our terms in the end, he had an important defense contract. Just when he thought he had it all sewn up, I put in a load more demands, he was practically bloody crying. On the way home he had a heart attack, drove right under the back of a bus, messy. The company went bust, I moved on, started it all over again somewhere else."

"You're not fit to be a representative of the workers." Sherry made no move to prevent it, as in upending the second bottle Gross tipped over backward in his chair. He managed to arrest his fall by clutching at the table, at the expense of several more smashed bottles.

"Workers? Don't make me laugh, I don't give a fuck about the workers." Walking unsteadily to the bar, Gross went behind it and relieved himself into a sink. "Who do you think it is who's been paying for the life of luxury I enjoy. I got a union job when I saw what a load of cloth-capped ignorant sods were in charge. Inside a couple of years I was earning more as a union official then most of the university educated wankers I was negotiating with, and all paid by the thick shits slaving their guts out on the factory floor. Bloody lovely, and even better when you add in the free car and petrol, expenses paid trips abroad, a mortgage through the union at a fixed two percent and not forgetting private health care insurance and last but not least those big fat fees from the TV stations every time I went to the studio and put on my serious-and-oh-so-deeply concerned-and genuinely-sorry face to lie about the reasons for yet another piddling stupid strike."

"You've had enough to drink."

"I have never had enough." Brushing aside Webb's attempt to wrest his bottle from him, Gross took a long series of gulps before paused for breath and then belching. "That's why I started taking Ivan's money. Easy it was, just start a strike here, rig a ballot there, nothing to it. I was doing it anyway, and the good old USSR paid up like I was doing it to order."

"Help me to carry Edwards to the car." Not really expecting any assistance, Webb was surprised when Gross, pants still gaping, took the professor's blanket-swaddled feet.

"Should have chucked him overboard like that ancient fool with the dog collar and worry beads." Having difficulty focusing as well as keeping his footing, Gross lurched in a zig-zag course with his share of their unconscious burden.

"Any further diminution of our numbers would, I feel, devalue our mission. In fact his condition might even enhance the propaganda value of our journey." Webb had to stop while the drunk disentangled his feet from the tangle of bandage that had unwound and was trailing from Edwards' right hand.

"How about if I slit his throat, then we'd have a heroic martryr, wouldn't we. That's got to be worth more points, hasn't it?" Giving up his attempts to divest himself of the bandage, Gross resigned himself to its hobbling restraint and signalled Webb to lead on. "Fucking silly idea. Did you fancy a bit of embalming practice?"

"I did it to stop him scratching himself, to lessen the chance of infection." Waiting for Sherry to unfasten the tailgate and move some of the equipment to make room, Webb's arms ached abominably when at last they were able to push the chemical's victim into the back of the Rover.

Much less gently, Gross swung his portion of the casualty inside, slamming shut the rear door without making any effort to arrange Edwards comfortably. "Well he's asleep isn't he? Christ," he became indignant at the looks the others gave him, "with all the problems he's got what difference is a ruddy stiff neck going to make?"

"You are an animal."

Breathing heavy alcoholic fumes over her, Gross nudged the woman. "Just parts of me. Want to see a cock that wouldn't disgrace a stallion?" His clumsy grab at her breast met only thin air as she stepped beyond his reach. Stuck up whore! He'd have her yet, every way he could, every way there was, and then some.

"Right, well I'll just collect the medical kit then, and we can be on our way." Webb pretended not to have seen the attempted indecent assault. The woman had a reputation, and if she didn't complain about the lout's advances then there was no reason for him to concern himself. And besides, she appeared quite capable of taking care of herself, and if he did intervene and it came to a physical conflict between him and Gross, he could not be certain of coming off best. Slight lingering qualms he might have had about leaving them together were allayed when the inebriate followed him back inside the inn.

"Thought I'd lay in a stock, to tide me over until we reach the commie lines and they top us up with vodka."

Webb half hoped the fall he heard on the cellar stairs meant Gross had sustained a disabling and painful injury, but the drunk heaved himself back to the bar a few minutes later smothered in cobwebs and burdened with many bottles.

"We don't have the room to take all those." The protest he made, Webb knew would be ineffectual.

"Oh piss off. With old Holy Joe gone there's loads of sodding room. If you still say there isn't then I'll chuck out the other old git." Blearily he examined a label. "Can't stand red, tastes like weak ink." He shied the bottle at a boar's head over the door, lurching unsteadily. "So far you've been giving all the orders, well from now on I want a say, and I say we get our priorities right. He waved a burgundy over his head before sending it at the candles. The room was darkened instantly, bottles clinked noisily. "These are my priorities."

Offering no further argument or resistance, Webb groped his way to the door. Glass crunched underfoot. All he could hope was that the uncouth Gross would swiftly drink himself into a stupor. The man's capacity for alcohol was legendary, but surely even he had to have a limit.

Watching him sprawl on the rear seat of the Rangerover, leaving the door for others to close, and start on a fresh bottle, Webb began to have doubts.

The food had gone cold, but Rozenkov didn't

notice, spearing a white dumpling that floated half submerged in the scum of grease on top of the fast congealing gravy, and pushing it and half the handle of the fork into his mouth. His jaws clamped tight and the prongs withdrawn were as bright as if just polished.

Beside him the radio chattered and crackled. He didn't miss a word, occasionally flicking the tuner to select another channel. It was not as good as being there himself, but it was the next best thing.

A timid knock at the door and a pink faced young junior sergeant entered, stopping yards short of the desk. He had to cough twice before he could speak. "The colonel has finished his meal?"

"Can you clean boots?"

Confused by the officer's unexpected question the soldier stumbled a hesitant affirmative.

"Good. When I take a new post I always like to start from scratch. You will look after me. I do not have time for petty detail. So long as my uniform is not crawling and my car is always ready when I want it, you should do. Can you manage that?"

"I think . . . Yes, Comrade Colonel."

"At last. You are the first in this building I have found prepared to commit himself. You can clear away . . . wait . . . this meal, who prepared it?"

"Sergeant-major Gorbatov, Comrade Colonel. You did not like it? He is usually very good, he was cook at our Washington embassy for five years. Very often he has cooked meals for . . ." Realizing he was being indiscreet he stopped abruptly.

"I know what you were going to say. Sometimes my predecessor would lend him out to party officials to

143

cater for private parties, in return for certain favors. Who is Gorbatov's assistant in the kitchens, what is he like, speak up man."

Any idea the junior sergeant might have had of softening or coloring the truth evaporated when the officer raised his voice. "It is Private Zhiraev, he . . . he is not a good cook. Gorbatov is always shouting at him. I think they are, that is I think they may be related, by marriage."

"And Sergeant-major Gorbatov, probably at the prompting of his wife or mother-in-law, is keeping the dolt here, far from the dangers of the front line. Another of the cozy arrangements that have been so much a feature of this department. Tell Private Zhiraev he is now in charge of the kitchens, tell him that as long as he does not poison anyone, without having been ordered to do so, he can ignore all complaints from my staff. He can refer them to me if they are persistent."

"What of Sergeant-major Gorbatov, Comrade Colonel."

"He is to report to Lieutenant General Akenshin at the department of satellite surveillance control at the ministry of defense."

Ignoring the soldier's departure with the tray. Rozenkov turned back to his map. Every thirty minutes during the afternoon Major Morkov had come in and moved the yellow markers a fraction to indicate the GRU units' latest reported positions. In a rough circle the lemon topped pins converged on the pencilled projected route the civilians were likely to travel, but they weren't closing quite as fast as he might have expected for such well equipped troops. And between two or three of the encircling companies there were larger than usual gaps.

"Get me Lieutenant General Akenshin at the defense ministry." Rozenkov continued to study the disposition of the yellow markers as he waited for the call to be connected. "Hello, Gregor, it's Rozenkov . . . Thank you. It is still subject to confirmation, but I think I shall yet make your exalted rank. Gregor, I have been able to do something for you. Do you still enjoy your love affair with your stomach . . . I thought so. I am sending you a chef I have discovered. Try him, you will not be disappointed . . . Well yes, there is something. If I give you some coordinates can you let me have a fast breakdown of activity in the immediate area, say within a hundred miles . . . The Zone, southern sector, Bavaria . . . You can? . . . Yes, ours and theirs, especially ours . . . Excellent, enjoy your meal."

As he replaced the receiver, Morkov came quietly into the room and working from scribbled notes on a pad moved each of the pins.

"Your men are spread more thinly than I'd expected, Major, even in that area. See, there are large gaps, here and here." Slouched in his chair, Rozenkov indicated where he meant by raising a leg and kicking at the locations, indenting the map into the soft plaster backing it.

Major Morkov sought any reason to be worried by those seemingly reasonable words. Though he found none, he began to perspire, and itch inside his smartly tailored uniform. "As the colonel must know, there are never enough men or vehicles to do everything precisely as we would wish to."

"Probably you are right, though I must admit, of late I have been gaining the distinct impression that the GRU has been obtaining all of its requirements and more, at the expense of KGB military units." Enjoying a thin smile at the liaison officer's difficulty in immediately refuting that, Rozenkov declined to go in for the kill, choosing to let his prey run a while longer. He saved the major from having to find an answer.

"No matter. If those are all the troops you have available, then they will have to do. I am sure you would produce more if you could."

Able to breathe again through a windpipe that nervous tension had constricted, Morkov made an excuse and left. In the corridor he paused to dab beads of water from his brow, and scrubbed the dampened handkerchief over his palms.

He could hear Rozenkov move about, and strained to hear what he was doing. For a moment he had half expected the colonel to come after him and order his arrest, it was with great relief that he heard the distinctive squeal of the drink cabinet being opened. So he was safe, and the overwhelming sensation of realizing that ruled out any further speculation as to what the head of Department A might be doing next.

It was tempting. Rozenkov held the red pin between thumb and forefinger, but finally decided to replace it in the hole it had occupied beside the map. It was too soon to make his move yet, he would hold his men back until the picture was clearer. At this stage he strongly suspected he was having to play the game without knowing the position of all his opponents' pieces. Such an advantage did not have to stay the monopoly of his adversary. The game was now more complicated, more dangerous.

CHAPTER ELEVEN

"They can have left only a few minutes ago, perhaps ten, not more." The reading Boris obtained from the infra-red detector was strong. Residual heat still radiated from the ground where the Rangerover had stood, and a higher level of emission from the ground below its engine even betrayed in which direction it had been parked.

"Damn." Revell didn't conceal his annoyance. He'd been counting on the civies calling a halt during the hours of darkness. "Ten minutes or ten hours, it makes no difference. That wagon of theirs can outrun us. We're never going to catch them in a tail chase."

"There's short cut we could take, Major." Using a hand-held torch to illuminate the map board, Hyde indicated a side road that turned off the autoroute to cut through the mountains and rejoin it forty kilometers further east. "Those civies have stuck to the main roads so far, doesn't seem too likely they'll change tactics in mid-course. If we can manage a decent speed over the high ground then we should come out in front of them, with time to arrange our own reception."

"Can we keep up speed?" There were attractions in the suggestion but the success or otherwise of the idea rested on whether or not the battle-weary APC was capable of maintaining the performance required.

Burke shrugged. "The engine's oil tight, and now it's thoroughly warmed up it's not running too bad. I've driven much worse further and faster. If we've already discovered the only weak link in the track, and if the transmission holds together, then we must be in with a chance."

It was his decision and his alone, Revell was very aware of that. If they lost the trail, for whatever reason; if the civies turned off before the roads rejoined, or if their rendezvous with their Russian friends was somewhere between here and the junction, then he'd failed.

But damn it, what ever arguments could be raised against the NCO's suggestion, it came back down to the fact that on present form their pursuit must fail. They couldn't count on the civilians stopping again. If they wanted a slice of good luck for a change they were going to have to cut it themselves.

"Okay, we take the turn-off."

During his deliberations Andrea had been beside him, occasionally leaning against him as she looked at the map. Her presence, her proximity made him feel good. A great effort of will, of self control would be involved, but he'd have to take things slow with her, not rush it.

It was probably by accident that Thorne's hand brushed against her breasts as he reached between them for a water bottle being passed around. Certainly Andrea made nothing of it, and she'd always been fast enough slapping aside any deliberate attempts to feel her body, but Revell reacted all the same.

"Keep your hands to yourself." Immediately he regretted his interference, wishing the engine had started a moment earlier and drowned his words. Still he was not sufficiently on guard over his jealousy, he would have to strive harder to keep it in check.

It had been a long time coming, longer than he'd expected, but it was no surprise to Clarence that Andrea had at last battened onto the major. Systematically she had worked through most of them, like an apprentice butcher eager to learn every aspect of the craft, how to cut and hack and mince flesh in a thousand different ways.

The Uzi submachine gun felt unfamiliar in his hands, and he glanced at the weapons rack to check that his Enfield sniper rifle was still safely secured. It swayed a little as the Marder lurched on turning off the autoroute onto the back road. The major's assault shotgun was next to it, its huge twenty round drum magazine dwarfing the grenade discharger barrel on Andrea's M16 next in line. Even their rifles were together.

Not that there was anything the officer could have done to speed the selection process, bring his turn faster. Andrea set her own pace, made her own rules.

The ride became rougher, and the Marder began to climb. The instruments indicating the level of contamination outside of their steel cocooned world, that had fallen dramatically since they left the gray woods, began to rise again.

As the angle of ascent became steeper Clarence had to exert considerable pressure on the bench and floor to prevent himself from sliding into Dooley. There was nothing he could do to stop Andrea from sliding into him.

The contact of the warm length of her thigh did nothing for him, no woman had, not since that Soviet Bomber had crashed on the married quarters in Cologne, and his wife . . . and children.

As so often they did, those thoughts drove all else from his mind and only gradually did he become aware that Revell was glaring at him. For a moment he didn't understand, then comprehension dawned as Andrea shifted slightly to a more comfortable position and he felt her move against him.

Ordinarily he would have wasted no time in distancing himself from that physical contact, but the major's attitude prompted him to uncharacteristic behavior, and he stayed where he was. The glare has deepened to a scowl, and to get away from it Clarence closed his eyes and leaned back against the hull feigning sleep.

In his mind he conjured pictures of the sort of country they were travelling through. His thoughts projected images of steep and rugged hillsides, often covered by dense forests of firs and pines, and in places gashed by deep river gorges and outcrops of frost shattered rock, and here and there, where the slope of the land was not so severe, a few cleared patches where farms clung to the valley sides. He had only to move his head a little, open his eyes and the image intensifying lens in his periscope would have enabled him to check the accuracy or otherwise of his imaginings.

The night was no impediment, the special glass would concentrate what little light there was and enable him to see as clearly as in day, but he didn't bother. He had seen enough of the Zone already.

Beyond the armored wall of the hull the landscape they passed did resemble the sniper's picture of it, the mountains and craps and cliffs and valleys were all there, but they lacked the furnishings of trees and grass and clear water he'd set on them. The basic contours of the land were there as they had been before the war, but there any similarity with the tourist brochures ended. Defoliants had stripped the trees of leaves and needles. No blade of grass remained, and with it had gone the patterns of the meadows that had marked out the farms. A few hardy, or miraculously fortunate plants survived, but now they looked alien in a panorama of lifeless decay where death was the norm.

With even their root systems shrivelled and destroyed by the constant showers of yellow rain and other Russian chemical weapons, the trees no longer bound the soil to the slopes and erosion on a gigantic scale was adding its contribution to the man-made havoc, silting and damming the rivers. Mud slides also blocked the road in places, and from the glutinous mounds projected lance-like lengths of snapped off timber.

Rarely shaving more than a fraction from their speed as he tackled each, Burke made scant allowance for the dangers of the slippery slopes. On one the tracks began to spin as loose material carried them toward a vertical drop to a debris-laden river several hundred feet below. They found traction again just in time, driving clear as part of the slide avalanched over the edge, taking a section of the road with it into the depths.

"Hell, I had my eyes closed then." Ripper left his periscope and reached to dig their driver in the back. "I ain't had a drive like this since I rode with my Uncle Billy hauling moonshine across the state line. He sure was in a hurry that day, Aunt Sarah had been denying him his conjugals for better than a month, on account of her being, like they say in the good book, kinda heavy with child."

"What did that have to do with his driving?" Scenting an interesting story in the offing, Dooley encouraged his fellow American.

"Well the fella we took the 'shine to, he always paid cash money on the barrel head, no fuss, no hassle. Uncle Billy planned to spend a goodly portion of it at Ma Kelly's. She ran a real smart brothel, over a Chinese laundry in Burford City, where we delivered. Aunt Sarah being to due to drop just about any time, Unc' was in a hurry to get back but wanted time for a couple of decent sessions before we had to turn about."

"Did you get his oats?" Thorne was taking a wry interest as well.

"Not that day. Snooping revenuers found a thimble-full of white lightning still in the tank under the back seat. In his hurry he got kinda careless. Didn't get his oats that or any day for quite a spell. I looked in on Ma Kelly's, though. That were the day I lost my virginity. I were just thirteen, but big for my years, if you catch my meaning."

Ripper had to pause there, as in attempting to nudge Dooley he moved the dressing on his arm. He rocked back and forth hugging the limb to him and keeping up an undertone of heartfelt obscenity.

"Well don't leave it there, tell us what happened." Dooley offered no vestige of sympathy, only encouragement to continue the story.

"Shit, that hurt. Think maybe this'll get me back stateside? Where was I?"

"Losing your virginity."

"Oh yeah. Soon as I stepped inside I was grabbed by this big red-head. Maybe she thought the bulge in my pants was a roll of money, or maybe not, anyway she hustled me into this room the size of a broom cupboard. I ain't kidding when I tell you if I'd been an inch taller we'd have had to do it standing up. So like a real pro she gets straight to the serious business first, and reels off a list of services and prices. She rattled through them too fast for me, shit, I'd have needed a medical dictionary to even figure what half of them were. When she asked me if I wanted to plate her I thought she were hinting she wanted me to help with the dishes."

"Get to it, what happened?" Leaning close in order not to miss anything, Dooley inadvertently crushed up against Ripper's sore arm and brought about another torrent of bad language, only at greater volume this time, and another delay.

"You do that again, you fat ox, and I won't tell you nothing. Like I was saying, I weren't sure what to do and she must have guessed I were just a learner 'cause she asked me if I'd ever seen dogs doing it. Hell, for us kids up in the hills watching the hounds make puppies was a spectator sport second only to peeping at grown-up cousins through knot holes in the barn when they were doing a spot of fingering. Only I didn't get time to tell her that, she went down on all fours, dragged her skirt up over her back and presented me with a target even a blind man couldn't have missed, 'cepting I got all nervous, poked twice and missed came too soon and turned her rump into the biggest cream slice you ever saw. Boy was she mad."

"That's put me off cake for life." With the conclusion of the story Thorne moved away.

"Not me." Dooley smacked his lips. "I'm into the first pastry shop I can find next leave I get."

"If you don't start using that bloody periscope and keep a watch for commie activity you won't be in a fit state to appreciate anything, that's if we get back." Hyde thrust spare magazines at Dooley.

"Aw come off it Sarge," Dooley had to get in the last word, "there won't be any Ruskies along this road. They'll only have a few units in the whole of this quarantined area and they'll all be raising dust trying to intercept those civies, trying to be the ones who get their picture in Pravda."

"And there was me, thinking Russians fought only for the glory of the motherland." Thorne was attempting an experiment with the flamethrower, seeing if he could align its broad nozzle to fire through one of the ball mounts.

"I thought there must be something wrong with your brain, all those warped bloody gadgets you keep coming up with, more likely to murder us than the fucking enemy." With disbelief Dooley watched the sapper trying to rig the improvised addition to the Marder's on-board defenses. "As for swallowing that bit about the Ruskies fighting for the motherland, that's a load of crap. Better than half the poor shits we're fighting aren't even bloody Russian, let alone commies. So far in this war I've fought with cruds conscripted from every country the Russians have grabbed in the past. I've stuck my bayonet in Cubans, Estonians, East Germans, Bulgarians, even a shitty shivering Angolan. All they were fighting for was to stay alive through one more day, waiting for a chance to desert without a KGB goon squad hauling them back and stomping their bollocks to mincemeat."

"Keep watching, Dooley," Revell put an edge on his voice, "or I'll be stamping on yours."

"On watch, Major. Watching now." Waiting until he was sure that the officer's attention had shifted elsewhere, he nudged Ripper. "In made to measure ambush country like this, if we do run into Russians, by the time I see them it'll be too bloody late!"

The information from the defense ministry was delivered directly into his hands, and the instant the door closed behind the messenger Rozenkov ripped the end from the large envelope.

It had been worth the two hour wait. He spread the borderless matte finished prints on the desk top and flicked through the typed sheets that accompanied them. Circled white letters were sprinkled across the photographs and of the location marked by each there was a separate enlargement, and a note among the listed information on the paperwork.

157

Swivelling around in his chair to face the map, the colonel checked off each against the yellow pins denoting GRU units, and almost immediately he found three military intelligence patrols Morkov had not told him about.

One of them was still too far from the civilians' probable route to pose any threat. Another was closer, but was having to traverse very bad going and offered no immediate danger to his plans. The third did, very definitely.

Even studying the appropriate enlargement, Rozenkov could not distinguish the detail for himself, but the notes said that the unit was composed of five armored vehicles, its radios were operating on frequencies reserved for the GRU and it was astride the autoroute the civilians were travelling, east of their last position. It was waiting for them.

Not for an instant did it occur to Rozenkov to speculate what urgent photographic interpretation work had been delayed while this favor had been done for him. The only matter that concerned him was his own position. If to hold that he had for a while to monopolize the entire resources of a stretched and overworked department, had to have the exclusive use of precious satellite surveillance time when elsewhere the outcome of whole battles might depend on other information it could have provided but didn't, then that was how it had to be.

He had seen other officers shot for failure in a minor mission of their own when they had sacrificed its success it enable a greater gain to be secured elsewhere. It was what he achieved that mattered to those above him, not what he assisted others to do, and so it was that his results were all that concerned him, nothing else.

A protest to the chief of Military Intelligence at the interference in his operation would be a total waste of time. Their friendship would count for nothing, not in a matter so important. General Mischenko would be very polite, very sympathetic, but he would deny all knowledge.

Raising his complaint with the men who had power over them both would be an even bigger mistake. Creating the impression that he was incapable of looking after the interests of his own department, and therefore of running it, the only result would be the utter ruin of his career prospects and his immediate removal and relegation to a position not half as senior as that he'd enjoyed at the Lubyanka.

Threats to Major Morkov could not succeed either. To resort to those would be tantamount to admitting to a more junior officer that events had got out of his control. No, if the operation was to be salvaged, if Department A alone was to get the rewards for its successful conclusion then it was he alone who would have to do the recovery work.

It was the right moment to bring the first of his pieces into the game. Although the map did not extend to cover the location where the crack KGB unit was waiting for orders, Rozenkov knew to the second what duration of flying time was involved to move it into play.

A glance at his unpretentious army issue watch told him that there was little time to spare. He reached for the radio and call sign and acknowledgment crackled back and forth over the air.

Giving the coordinates first, he waited for them to be repeated; this was not going to fail because of trivial mistakes that should never have happened.

". . . and you do understand what is required? Good. Leave this channel open, I shall wish to listen."

Perhaps it was actually static or a fault in the tuner or speaker, but Rozenkov fancied he could hear the gunships' engines and main rotors screaming to full power . . .

CHAPTER TWELVE

"We are outnumbered and outgunned." Andrea crouched behind the fungus blotched trunk of a fallen tree, and watched the activity about the Soviet armored cars and personnel carriers.

That was a conclusion that Revell had already been forced to accept. If they were really lucky, and managed to get close enough they might knock out one or two of the big enemy vehicles, perhaps disable another, but the answer to any surprise success they had would be swift and overwhelming.

It was only by chance they'd avoided driving straight into the formidable road block. They had stopped shortly before rejoining the autoroute, to secure loose equipment drumming on the exterior of the Marder's hull. Boris had taken the opportunity to make a fast infra-red sweep from the vantage point of the top of the turret and the instrument had detected the rising heat from from the Russian's engines and exhausts.

Showing as a pink glow drifting over the tree tops, it had registered with sufficient definition for a bearing to be taken. It had taken little thought on Revell's part to elect himself to go and investigate, taking Andrea with him.

The enemy vehicles were parked haphazardly across the autoroute, but effectively blocked its full width, not more than a few hundred yards beyond where the detour rejoined it. A few troops had dismounted, mostly officers, and dressed in full NBC gear with the exception of respirators they strolled about casually.

Senior among them appeared to be an officer with a zoom-lens fitted Pentax slung by a cord about his neck. Every now and again he would lift it and squint down the road through its viewfinder.

"That's a reception party. I was expecting them to drag along a gaggle of news men and a film crew, but there's no doubt who they're waiting for. Looks like we managed to get in front of the civies, but just a little late." A noise that Revell had at first attributed to an auxiliary charging engine or generator aboard one of the armored cars, now began to intrude more upon his hearing. It was becoming louder, getting closer, and was joined by a second.

"Helicopters!" Through a gap in the leafless interwoven branches overhead, Andrea pointed to an orange stutter of exhaust flame in the sky. "They are circling."

"Either they're lost, or they're looking for something. Could be a few Party bosses come to spice up the welcome committee, or maybe the press contin-

162

gent I was expecting. This lot'll put up a flare for them in a moment."

"Then what is your plan? Do we sit here and wait until the traitors arrive, and then watch their Russian friends put their propaganda machine into action?"

"You'd attack the roadblock I suppose, put a grenade into the gut of that Russian officer."

"No, I would put a grenade into the civilians' transport when it arrived. From here it will be an easy target. Using an incendiary shell there will be no mistake, no survivors."

Revell had noticed earlier the color coded tip of the shell she'd loaded into the underslung launcher. "And you're all ready to do just that, aren't you."

"Of course. There is not the time for us to get to them first. Our orders are to prevent them reaching the Russians. How else would we do that now?"

On the road the Russian drivers had remounted, and guided by directions from their officers were backing the cumbersome vehicles off the metalled surface and under the trees, except for a command version of an eight wheeled APC that was proving reluctant to restart.

The troop's response to the approach of the aircraft didn't make sense. Revell's first reaction was to doubt his identification of the choppers, but he had been forced too often in the past to take cover from attacks by Soviet gunships to mistake their distinctive engine beat. With nothing logical on which to base a judgment, all he had was intuition, and a gut feeling told him what had to be done.

"Put a shell into that stalled eight-wheeler."

Of all the orders she might have received, that was

the one that Andrea had been least expecting. She didn't question it, but there was a perceptible hesitation before she fired, as though subconsciously she was giving the major an opportunity to countermand it.

With the range barely a hundred yards, the grenade's trajectory was virtually flat and it skimmed the surface of the road to impact and burst on the side of the command vehicle low on its hull between its big rear wheels.

Spikes of white light engulfed the APC and spitting balls of phosphorus that failed to lodge in the deep treaded tires bounced off to form a carpet of blazing globules.

Amid shouting and confusion a Russian officer ran with waving arms to the other vehicles and hammered on their armor, trying vainly to attract the attention of their crews to get them to cease the heavy indiscriminate fire they were sending into the trees. He went unheard or ignored as the storm of zipping tracer ricocheted between the trunks and in their display dwarfed the already diminishing fire about the command vehicle.

"Time to get out of here." Without further explanation Revell grabbed Andrea's arm and began to tow her at speed back to the Marder.

"They are not firing at us, let me go, I do more damage to them."

"Don't argue, just run."

Their way faintly and erratically illuminated by the flames from a tire that had taken hold, above the crackling and crashing of heavy machine gun and cannon fire came another sound. Passing directly above them, it reached a crescendo as a violent downdraft blasted pine needles, cones and twigs at them. Temporarily blinded by the stinging wind-born debris, Revell kept going, keeping a tight hold on Andrea and accepting the painful collisions with unseen trees as they blundered on.

He regained his vision as night was washed from the forest and replaced first by a glaring red and then by a brilliant white light that painted the lifeless ground with the sharp dark shadows of the pines.

The blast wave that struck them was a hundred times stronger than that from the helicopters' spinning rotors, and it was hot, a lung-hurting roasting heat that made every breath a sharp sensation.

Without time to take cover, they were hit by a hammer-hard wall of fast-moving air that was pushing down trees before it and joined the splintered timber in crashing to the ground where a deluge of light material piled against them in a drift.

Close behind its leader, the second gunship dumped two more super-napalm cannisters, but with greater accuracy, using the vivid fire among the trees caused by the first strike to correct its aim.

The tumbling petrol-jelly filled drop tanks hit the autoroute alongside the disabled eight-wheeler and by the glare of the orange and yellow flame that enveloped it, its companion vehicles could be seen.

From every hatch and door jumped their crews and infantry passengers but none of them made more than a couple of paces before the second stage ignition occurred. At the center of the fireball, even as it began to rise and contract, to roll and suck in upon itself, the oxygen cylinders that had spilled

165

from the cannister on impact ruptured and multiplied the temperature and area of combustion.

White furnace flame enveloped the Russians and consumed them. Grenades and small arms ammunition exploded instantly, and those spitting heaps, topped by dense black smoke from burning gas capes and respirators were all that marked where each had fallen when the enhanced fireball lifted above the trees.

Each of the armored cars and APCs blazed fiercely, spirals of fire coming from every opening and the many splits in their overpressure ripped hulls.

There was little time for the helicopter pilots and gunners to congratulate themselves on the results of their strike. Perhaps the lead ship turned too sharply or the following craft a shade too late, but whichever it was the effect was as catastrophic for them both.

Whirling blades sliced apart a cabin and tail-boom as they came together. Sparks, in a rapid series of huge showers, marked the mid-air collision and at the moment of contact the tearing metal produced a noise that smothered that of the fires on the ground.

For the lead ship the end came fast. Rotor blades reduced to whistling stumps, it plummeted like a stone. The red mushroom that flared briefly to mark where it went in was puny compared to those it had helped create only seconds earlier.

Severely damaged but still under a degree of control the other gunship began a staggering descent, its progress marked clearly in the night sky by the long flare from an exhaust that had been stripped of its shielding cowl. That ceased abruptly when both engines cut out together, and from five hundred feet it side-slipped to destruction away to the east.

They back-tracked for six kilometers along the autoroute before they found where the civilians had turned off. Five minutes along that side road and they came upon the wreckage of the second gunship to crash.

Dooley had managed to avoid being selected as one of those to go out and make a quick search of the site, and he made the most of it, sprawling at full length and enjoying the rare luxury of being able to do so within the vehicle's cramped interior. "I bet you anything you like that those civies saw the fireworks, got the shits and are heading back home." He spoke to the squad in general, but his eyes were on Andrea as she brushed soil from her smock. As her hands passed over the voluminous garment they smoothed it to the full contours of her body.

"You're on. How about a hundred marks."

Their driver's too ready acceptance of the bet made Dooley deeply suspicious, and he hesitated. "Do you know something I don't?"

"Lots, and especially that our civie friends may have turned off the main road, but they're still heading east. Stubborn lot of sods, aren't they."

"Maybe they've an extra reason now." Hyde climbed in, handed a bundle of papers to the major and took his place on the bench by the rear door. "They've lost one of their number already, and we know they've got at least one more in a bad way. There were all those bandage wrappings at the inn. Perhaps they're thinking that their best chance is to get medical help from the Reds."

"Translate these, Boris." Revell handed the stained documents to their Russian radio man.

Boris turned the pay books over in his hand. They were sticky, many of the pages were stuck together by congealing blood. "Are these from the crew of the helicopter?"

"Crew or passengers, it's impossible to tell." With a scrap of cloth Sergeant Hyde scrubbed his fingers. "The way that crate piled in there's hardly anything left that's identifiable. Took those from bodies that had been thrown clear, those still in the wreck are partially buried with it. Metal and meat, all tangled together, very messy, and smelly."

"I want to know if there's any clue to be got from them as to why commie gunships have started bouncing their own ground troops." Revell waited impatiently as the pages were carefully peeled apart.

By the poor light of a single low powered red bulb, Boris examined the cryptic entries that gave details of the slab faced men whose pictures were pasted inside the stiff front covers.

"This one belongs to a KGB major, a political officer; this to a member of a KGB film unit, a cameraman." He opened the last. "And this was taken from a KGB medical officer. In the back there is a list of courses he has attended. The last mentions chemical and biological warfare."

Taking the papers, Hyde fanned them like a hand of cards. "That's a pretty high powered outfit, not the sort you'd expect to find stooging about in a chopper at night, over the quietest part of the Zone, using the rest of the Red Army for ground attack practice."

"Don't make no sense to me neither." Ripper was taking a chance. Playing on his wound he'd managed to avoid being allocated any work, so far. By butting in he risked that, but he hadn't spoken for ten minutes, and couldn't resist the temptation. "Hell, if the KGB are figuring on barging in on someone else's show, all they had to do was land and tell the poor shits to bugger off. They always get their own way, don't they, so why toast the creeps."

"Perhaps they could not be sure of getting their own way, and that was their method of ensuring they did." It was the first time Boris had seen super napalm in use. What made it even more terrible than in the instance he had witnessed, it had been used by Russians on Russians. "Often there is intense rivalry between the KGB and other specialist units, like Military Intelligence, the GRU. Always they are at each other's throats. Fights are common in the bars and brothels when they meet."

"There's a heck of a difference between a rough house over a whore, and dumping liquid hell on a whole parcel of your own people."

Boris dismissed Ripper's objection. "Not to men of their type, dedicated communists. The headquarters of both the KGB and GRU are in Moscow. As much as they must strive to succeed themselves, they must work to see that others don't. If the prize is big enough, of sufficient importance then they will not hesitate to do what you have seen tonight."

In the absence of any more plausible theory Revell had to accept that. "Okay, if that's how it is then maybe it's a break for us. If they're scrapping among themselves it could mean their effort is going to be halved."

"If they're both searching for the civies," a thought struck Ripper, "could mean their effort is gonna be doubled instead . . ." He had to duck, shielding his arm as an assortment of equipment was hurled at him.

"I tell you, you got to stop."

Webb wrenched the wheel over and the power steering sent the Rangerover in a tight tire-scrubbing turn off the road. "What for?" Jabbing his foot hard on the brake pedal he brought the vehicle skidding to a gravel-scattering halt beside a picturesque log cabin. Several more were spaced out among the trees, linked by a network of rambling paths to a large two story building of similar construction that formed the center of the holiday complex.

Sherry didn't answer, throwing open the door, gulping air and then walking unsteadily to sit on the steps leading to a raised veranda that ran the length of the front of the cabin. "Jesus, I ain't ever been travel sick before. Oh god, I think I'm going to throw up."

"I'll join you." Gross tumbled and lurched from the back of the Rover to spew noisily beside it, coughing and spitting loudly when he'd finished. "Must be all the fucking bubbles that do it for me. How those bloody chinless wonders can swill that champagne muck all night and day I'll never know."

Retching was all that Sherry could achieve, even with that revolting display only yards from her. Unable to prevent them she gave a series of loud belches

170

that the back of her hand only partially smothered, but afterward her stomach felt more settled.

"Better?" Wiping his mouth on his sleeve, Gross plonked down beside her. "I knew a fat tart once who did that, not with her mouth though." He tried to put his arm around Sherry, but she shrugged him off and got up. Rising unsteadily, Gross joined her in leaning on the balcony rail. "And I don't mean her mouth either." From a distended pocket he tugged a bottle, and after a wrestle to extract the cork, took a long pull at it. "When we had it off, always in the good old missionary position, I had this trick of almost withdrawing at the end of each thrust. By the time the old juices were ready to flow I'd have her pumped full of air. Soon as I'd finished and climbed off she'd shove her hands down hard on her gut and out it'd all come again." Not deterred by the first rebuff, he tried again to put his arm over her shoulders.

"You touch me again and I'll stomp your balls off."

"Say that again. I like it when you talk dirty. At home I've got a video of that scene where the black tries to bugger you in that shop doorway, and you tell him what he can do with his tool. That's a favorite of mine." Offering the bottle, Gross had it pushed back at him.

"Get lost."

Impatient at the delay, Webb left the driving seat and brought the woman a drink of water. He carefully peeled the lid from the Tupperware beaker before handing it to her. "We are wasting time. Are you ready to go again yet?"

"Oh what's up, Webby." Pouring a drop of wine on the withered stump of a begonia in a window box,

Gross peered closely at it, squinting to see it in the dark, as if expecting an elixir quality in the Mosel to immediately restore it to full bloom. "Did that little bit of excitement up ahead earlier get you just a teensy bit frightened? Don't you like bonfires?"

"All I want is to make it safely to our destination. I am worried about Edwards' condition. We need him alive to retain the maximum credibility of our mission. Our message will be devalued if his name is not on it also."

"Bollocks." Holding the bottle high, Gross jiggled it and then put it to his ear to try to determine how much remained of its contents. "The old windbag was devalued years ago, when all his arse-holing chums at university were exposed in the British Sunday press. From what I read it'd seem that when those cap and gowned queers weren't trying to spawn another commie cell they were frantically trying to spawn each other. Between planting agents with bogus degrees in the British civil service and buggering the piles out of their students I wonder they ever had time to give lectures."

"Well we still cannot stay here, it might not be healthy."

"That at least makes more sense than the crap you came out with before." With all the force he could muster, Gross threw the empty bottle through a small window in the chalet door. "Come on Kane, stop bloody heaving. Your tits wobble every time you do it and I'm going to spunk in my pants if you don't stop."

Wheezing snores came from the back of the Rangerover. Webb listened before starting the engine.

"Does he sound congested to you? There are some marks on his face, do you think he might have swallowed some?"

"If he has then it won't matter how soon we get help for the daft old sod, he's had it." Gross sought among the bottles on the floor for a full one. "Back in the seventies I did a stint on an industrial injuries tribunal, dealt with a few cases of accidents in chemical plants. Get any of that muck inside you and it rots your insides, especially if it goes into your lungs. Infection sets in and you drown in your own pus."

Everything else Sherry Kane had been able to cope with, Gross being violently ill, his filthy stories; but the picture that last information conjured was too much, and she barely got her head out of the window in time.

The notes Webb had made before starting out told him to expect sunrise at a few minutes after seven. It was nearer nine o'clock before they became aware of a perceptible lightening of the sky ahead, and that was muted by the suspended dust through which the orb of the sun only faintly showed.

For Sherry it would have been better if it had waited a further hour before shedding its weak light on the ravaged land. They drove into a small town that only needed a wave of a wand to restore it to bustling life again.

Whatever had struck the inhabitants had struck very fast, without hint of warning. There was nothing to suggest that any warning had been broadcast, any precautions taken or panic started.

A bus and a few trucks partially obstructed the main street. Some had coasted to a gentle stop, but several had been in collisions, with each other, with shop fronts, with trees. The Rangerover had frequently to be driven onto the pavement to negotiate the enforced slalom course. In every cab they passed they saw the same sight.

Draped over steering wheels, sprawled across passenger seats were the vehicles' drivers. Most were miraculously preserved inside their glass and steel mausoleums, others, where windows were down, were decomposed to varying repulsive degrees.

And there was worse. No vegetation had grown to hide what lay in the streets and playgrounds. The yards of the schools were thick with the skeletal remains of children, rows of larger bones and skulls outside a bakery marked where a food queue had succumbed. Still strapped in a pushchair, mummified and eyeless, the tiny frame of a baby.

"I don't want to see any more. Tell me when it's gone." Putting her face in her hands Sherry could try to pretend that the town of the dead did not exist, but she knew it was there still, she could hear bones crunching under the wheels, could feel the bumping as they rode over skulls that collapsed under the vehicle's weight.

Only slowly did it register that a hand had come over the seat back, on over her shoulder and after a consoling pat in pretense of administering comfort was trying to find a way inside her shirt.

For a while she made no move to stop its groping progress as it rubbed and pinched and squeezed the

174

contours of her chest, then still in the same trance-like state of shock she reached for it, lifted it gently to her lips, and sank her teeth into it.

Gross's screamed obscenity drowned the loud hiss of escaping air as a razor-sharp shard of hip bone pierced a tire.

FROM M16 THROUGH CIA LONDON. FOR DISTRIBUTION TO ALL SECTIONS:
STATE DEPARTMENT, PENTAGON. TOP COPY FOR PRESIDENT.

ROZENKOV. YURI NIKOLAI. COLONEL. KGB.

JOINED COMMUNIST YOUTH MOVEMENT 1939. PARTY MEMBER 1942. VOLUNTEERED FOR ARMY SPRING 1943. SELECTED FOR NKVD AFTER COMPLETION OF BASIC TRAINING AT CAMP 1094. PROMOTED TO JUNIOR SERGEANT IN JANUARY 1945. MEMBER OF THE RAIDING PARTY SENT INTO BERLIN TO SECURE THE FILES AT GESTAPO HQ BEFORE THEY COULD BE DESTROYED. DECORATED TWICE FOR VALOR. AFTER THE WAR WORKED ON THE EIGHT FLOOR OF KGB HEADQUARTERS AT 2, DZHERZHINSKIY SQUARE, IN THE OFFICE DEALING WITH THE TRANSLATION AND EVALUATION OF CAPTURED DOCUMENTS. PROMOTED TO SERGEANT 1952 ON JOINING 3RD. BATTALION, FIRST DZHERZHINSKIY MOTORIZED DIVISION, RESPONSIBLE FOR THE GUARDING OF GOVERNMENT BUILDINGS IN MOSCOW. WAS ON LEAVE WHEN THE ATTEMPTED COUP BY BERIA FAILED IN 1953. SURVIVED THE PURGES OF THE UNIT.

1956/7 WAS ATTACHED TO THE RUSSIAN LIAISON

STAFF WITH THE EAST GERMAN INTELLIGENCE DIREC-
TORATE (HVA) WITH THE RANK OF SERGEANT-MAJOR.
ASSISTED WITH THE RUNNING OF AN INDUSTRIAL ESPIO-
NAGE NETWORK IN WEST GERMANY, USING EX-NAZIS
COOPERATING UNDER THREAT OF EXPOSURE. SPRING
1958 WENT TO OFFICER TRAINING ACADEMY AT KIEV
AND FROM THERE TO THE KGB "FINISHING SCHOOL"
(CORRECT DESIGNATION UNKNOWN) AT GAGZINKA.
POSTED TO THE ADMINISTRATION SECTION OF THE STAFF
OF THE POLITICAL DIRECTORATE WITH THE RANK OF
LIEUTENANT IN SEPTEMBER 1961.

1968 APPEARED IN CUBA WITH THE RANK OF CAP-
TAIN, AND WORKING UNDER AMBASSADOR ALEKSAN-
DRE ALEKSEYEVICH SOLDATOV MASTERMINDED THE
PURGE OF THE CUBAN SECRET POLICE OF ELEMENTS NOT
SLAVISHLY LOYAL TO THE MOSCOW LINE. APPOINTED
SECOND IN COMMAND OF THE INTERROGATION TRAIN-
ING WING OF THE KGB SCHOOL IN '69. ATTENDED
STAFF COURSE AT LENINGRAD DURING 72/73. PRO-
MOTED MAJOR IN 1974 AND GIVEN COMMAND OF A KGB
SPETSNAZNACHENIYA (SPECIAL DESIGNATION) UNIT
WITH UNDEFINED DUTIES, BELIEVED TO BE AN EXECU-
TION, ASSASSINATION AND "DIRTY JOBS" SQUAD OF
PICKED OFFICERS AND NCOs. IT IS REPORTED THAT
UNDER HIS GUIDANCE THE TECHNIQUE OF ASSASSINA-
TION BY STAGED MOTOR ACCIDENTS WAS PERFECTED.
AMONG VICTIMS OF THE METHOD HE DEVISED ARE
THOUGHT TO BE THE DISSIDENT IRINA KAPLUN, EDITOR
OF AN UNDERGROUND NEWSPAPER IN ESTONIA AND THE
EXILE ANDREI AMALRICK, A SOVIET HISTORIAN, IN
SPAIN. ROZENKOV WOULD HAVE BEEN CONSULTED
WHEN THE SAME METHOD WAS USED TO ELIMINATE
PYOTR MASHEROV, COMMUNIST PARTY CHIEF OF

BYELORUSSIA AND A POLITBURO CANDIDATE MEMBER, WHEN HE WAS SUSPECTED OF PLANNING A GRAB FOR POWER IN THE EARLY EIGHTIES.

APART FROM A BRIEF APPEARANCE IN EARLY '82 WHEN HE WAS IDENTIFIED AS ONE OF THE COLONELS FOLLOWING THE COFFIN OF KREMLIN IDEOLOGIST MIKHAIL SUSLOV, HE FELL FROM SIGHT, REAPPEARING IN NOVEMBER 1982 AS GOVERNOR OF THE LUBYANKA PRISON AND INTERROGATION CENTER. HE HAS HELD THE POSITION, WITH ONE ABSENCE TO ATTEND A FURTHER STAFF COURSE UNTIL HIS RECENT APPOINTMENT AS HEAD OF DEPARTMENT A OF THE FIRST CHIEF DIRECTORATE OF THE KGB.

IT IS BELIEVED THAT HE IS NOT YET CONFIRMED IN THE POST, USUALLY HELD BY A GENERAL, AND AT PRESENT RETAINS THE RANK OF COLONEL.

FULL EVALUATION FOLLOWS. SUMMARY. ROZENKOV IS AN EXPERIENCED CAREER KGB OFFICER OF PROVEN ABILITY. IT CAN BE EXPECTED THAT UNDER HIS COMMAND THE DEPARTMENT WILL BE HIGHLY ACTIVE.

CHAPTER THIRTEEN

Static hissed from the radio. Rozenkov had not bothered to switch it off. He'd heard the pilot's shouts of alarm and then terror as the helicopters had collided, and then the terrified howling of their crews as they'd plunged to the ground.

A moment before he'd received the codeword signalling a successful strike, but it wasn't the loss of the gunships and their crews that had taken the edge from his satisfaction with the destruction of the GRU roadblock. Soon after had come word that the civilians had altered course and were now heading directly toward another Military Intelligence patrol.

With hindsight Rozenkov could wish he'd put more KGB units into the field, but there was nothing he could do about that now. He would have to accept that he was suddenly reduced to one piece, and that from here on it would be necessary for him to play with every shred of his skill and cunning.

179

Major Morkov burst into the room. His face was flushed and sweat stood out on his forehead as he thumped his fist down hard on the desk. "The order came from you. It could only have come from you."

"Calm yourself, Comrade Major." Rosenkov pretended ignorance. "If you will tell me what you think I have ordered to be done, I shall tell you whether you are correct or not. It is not possible for me to admit to, or deny any accusation the details of which I am not aware."

From a drawer he took a miniature Japanese tape recorder and switched in on. "Proceed, feel free to repeat what you have just said, in the same tone if you wish." Folding his hands over his stomach and swivelling gently back and forth in his chair, he waited.

Morkov hesitated. As a matter of course he knew that all conversation in the room would be taped, but the ostentatious use of the personal recorder warned him to be especially on his guard. Word had come from General Mischenko himself that the protest was to be made in the strongest possible manner, with a show of indignation and anger, and in doing that he knew he could count on his chief's protection, but this was Rozenkov's home ground, and already he was laying traps.

Not eager to be the one to spring them and learn and suffer the consequences, Morkov decided to cover himself, make sure that he stayed well within the limits of the extent of that protection. In a dead-pan monotone he delivered the gist of the complaint with no more feeling than he would have employed in asking the way to the lavatory.

"I report that field company one-four-nine of Military Intelligence Command, on temporary attachment to Tenth Guards Army, southern sector, Zone, has suffered heavy casualties while operating in conjunction with and under the direction of Department A of the KGB."

"That is most interesting, Major. Can you tell me, precisely what are the casualty figures?"

"Preliminary reports are vague, but it would appear . . . that the unit has ceased to exist, Comrade Colonel."

"Then it would seem that the casualties are very heavy indeed. I presume in that case that there are no eye witnesses to the attack." Getting no response, Rozenkov drove relentlessly on. "Would the unit be one of those you have indicated on my map?" Still there was nothing from the liaison officer. "Ah, then their loss will not affect the outcome, the successful outcome, of this KGB operation."

"No . . . Comrade Colonel." The words near choked him. It had been a trap, but so carefully prepared and concealed that he was snared before he even knew it was there.

As he left the room he was already planning his next move. If word of this ever leaked to Military Intelligence GHQ, then it would do him no good at all. To outweigh that, if it should ever happen, it was more vital than ever that he turn the whole operation to the advantage of the GRU. Whatever the risk, whatever the cost, he must make sure it was a unit under his control that intercepted the civilian peace delegation.

This was not the time for finesse, for subtlety, it was determined and if need be ruthless action that was called for. Speed was of paramount importance but he no longer dared use the scrambler phone in his office in this building. There was an unwritten agreement between the two intelligence agencies that a liaison officer's communications with his HQ should not be intercepted, but Morkov was a realist in a harsh world and was aware that if the line was not already bugged, it would be soon.

Leaving the building would be reported to Rozenkov, and regarded with suspicion but there was no choice. For what he was setting in motion he needed to be certain of utter secrecy. The only way he could feel confident of that was by returning in person to GRU headquarters and using their transmitter.

When he reached the exit the five minute wait while his car was summoned from the motor pool was agonizing. For fear of being overheard by the white gloved KGB guard who sprang forward to open the door for him, and was slow in closing it, he waited until they were moving into the traffic flow before instructing his driver.

From the picture window of his top floor office, from behind two inches of armor glass that slightly distorted the view, Rozenkov watched the liaison officer's hurried departure, and that of the anonymous gray Moskvich saloon that followed at a discreet distance. The tail was hardly necessary, he could be quite certain as to where the major was heading, but he had already learned the hard way not to underestimate the man's ambition; he was not about to make the same mistake over his desperation.

Leaving the window, he crossed to his desk and picked up the internal telephone. His own operator responded instantly, but there was a perceptible delay before the section he asked for answered. He made a mental note for future reference and action.

"Rozenkov . . . I shall want a transcript of all transmissions from GRU headquarters made in the next hour. Have them sent to me as fast as they are decoded . . . then get the extra men you need!" He made another note, and the need for a shake-up of the Radio Traffic Interception section moved higher in his list of priorities, taking second place behind the obtaining of a GRU liaison officer.

"Pity those bloody civies didn't stay put in that holiday village, or whatever it was. If they had we'd have been on our way home by now." On the major's instruction Burke had slowed the Marder to a walking pace as the road topped a ridge, and brought it to a halt in a hull-down position while the officer, their NCO and the girl went forward to reconnoiter the route ahead.

"Anybody want a hand of cards while we're waiting?" Rippling the thick greasy deck, Dooley looked around, but there were no takers. "Come on you mean bastards. You can't take it with you."

"Ain't that the truth." Swallowing the antibiotic and painkiller Thorne had handed him, Ripper pulled a face at the plastic tainted taste of the tepid water he used to wash them down. "But if I ain't takin' it with me, I sure don't see any reason for makin' a gift of it to you before I go."

Taking care not to bump the wide lens of the powerful infra-red camera against the sides of the hatch, Boris lowered it to the bench, before climbing down himself and starting to stow the equipment.

"Managed to get any good dirty pictures with that recently? Anything saleable?" Reluctantly returning the cards to his pocket, Dooley took out a well-thumbed back copy of Forum and began to flick through it, having to squint closely to see the detail of small photographs illustrating an article on lesbianism. "If you could use all that fancy gear to get a few shots like this," he held the small booklet open towards the Russian, "we could make a few bucks. You know, that's a business I wouldn't mind going in for when I get out."

"I thought you were off to Florida to offer your services to all the wrinkled old widows. There can't be much of a market for pictures of them." Burke shuddered at the thought. "Horrible, all wispy gray hair and sagging tits."

"Yeah, well I am still going there, but I can have a sideline can't I?" In the poor light of the compartment Dooley was having to strain his eyes to see the pages, and gave up. "Anyway, I don't go for the real elderly crows, just the nice plump mature ones, those still able to remember what it was like, and fancy a refresher course with an Adonis like me."

"I think you can forget about doing either."

Watching the contamination monitor, Clarence saw it edge a fraction higher as a gust of wind buffeted the APC on the exposed ridge. Another couple of points and they would have to put on the respirators. The prophylactics they took in such quantities could not be guaranteed to work in so polluted an atmosphere. "We would just be lying to ourselves if we ever imagined we're going to get out of the Zone, except in a box."

"You're wrong." Revell stamped the dust from his overshoes before entering. "Looks like the Russians let fly with all this chemical muck without licking their fingers to test which way the wind was blowing. Some of it came right back in their faces. This saturated area extends much further on their side than they've admitted. There's a village just over the hill, and it's definitely not West German. A couple of miles back we must have crossed into Czechoslovakia. Did the infra-red camera register anything interesting?"

He'd been waiting to be asked, and Boris handed over the clearest of the three frames he had taken. The heat sensitive film had captured the small town in merging shades of muted red and blue. Some particularly distinctive individual buildings, like churches, could be identified, but of much more interest was the sprinkling of darker red spots, most of them on their own, but some in clusters, or lines. "I tried to count them, but there are so many?"

"What are they?" Having pushed in for a look, Andrea found she could not interpret the images.

"Well a couple of them might be weak sunlight

185

reflecting from glass, or bare metal. That large one," Boris indicated a red smudge, "is a petrol station. The underground storage tanks hold heat quite efficiently. But most of them are bodies. Decomposition will be keeping their flesh at a higher temperature than their surroundings. Those registering most strongly will be inside vehicles, be rotting more slowly."

"That is excellent. For once the war has been carried behind the iron curtain. I am pleased." Without asking she took the picture and examined it closely, trying to estimate the number of dead. "The Russians and their puppets have so far always fought the war beyond their own borders, I am very happy that this time their people have suffered."

"You evil bitch." Clarence could have hit her. "Those aren't combat troops lying down there, that's women and children."

"The communists have never hesitated to slaughter indiscriminately, you know that better than most, your own family . . ."

"Be quiet, don't say it."

Although the sniper said the words so softly they were hardly a whisper, Andrea stopped in mid sentence. They looked at each other, her overspilling hatred meeting his coldly calculated determination, and each found its match.

"Shouldn't we be moving?" Ripper lay between the two silent antagonists and the tension over him was like an axe poised to drop. "Hey, now don't you start nothing, I'm in the middle. See, I'm wounded."

It was Andrea who broke the deadlock, but not to

finish what she had been saying. Her voice was almost mechanical in its delivery. "There is no longer any hurry. Only one road leaves the town on the far side, and it is under water. The traitors will be going no further, we have only to go and . . . collect them?"

Revell had been about to intervene when Ripper had spoken first, now he was glad he'd not. Inevitably he would have sided with her, and it would not have gone unnoticed. Even the eye contact that she and the sniper had maintained for so long had torn at him. "Let's go. I want all ports manned. Thorne, get into the turret and pull the co-ax machine gun. Try rigging the flamethrower for use from there. The hoses should reach if you take it easy with the traverse. I haven't seen any, but it's possible the commies were waiting for them down there. I don't want us to bumble unprepared into any welcoming party that might be in progress."

"Don't worry, Major." Once again the bulky cylinders caused havoc and confusion as they were dragged half the length of the cramped interior by Thorne. "If they are, I'll hot things up for them."

"There they are." Burke was first to spot the Rangerover, parked in the middle of the road a hundred yards ahead.

A figure crouched beside the vehicle and as they approached stood, took a cautious step back, then hesitantly waved. Still clutching a wheel brace he held that half welcoming, half nervous pose then as the distance between him and the approaching APC shortened he saw the faded West German emblem on the Marder's front, threw down the tool and ran.

"After him."

The moment it took them to throw open the heavy rear door, and the penalty of having to run in the cumbersome NBC suits was too great a disadvantage to overcome. The man took the steps of a church four at a time and slammed the massive iron studded door before the squad reached the foot of the flight.

"Shit, this place is built like a fortress." Dooley ran his hand over the large stone blocks of which the church was fashioned.

Hyde and Revell took it in turns to shout through the stout double doors in an attempt to persuade the civilians to come out.

"Our arrival must have come as a shock," Clarence sat on the steps. "After having come this far, I can't see them just tamely going back with us. They'll simply sit tight and wait for their Russian chums to locate them."

"That seems to be about the size of it." Getting no response to his calls, Revell ceased, and stepped back to look up at the building's high-set windows. "We can't afford to hang around for long, but the orders said to use kid gloves, so we'll give it a last try. In the meantime, back the Marder into a side alley, no point in advertising where we are to any sky-spies that the Ruskies send over. Check for another way into this place while I spell out the alternative to these damned civies."

As he turned to the door again he realized that

Andrea was close by his side. He liked her there, but he knew what her automatic response would be as soon as entry was gained. She would start shooting, and he couldn't let that happen. "You stay with the Marder."

Andrea knew why Revell ordered that, and began to protest, but checked herself. Understanding his reasoning did not make it any easier to accept. Learning the skills of command was not going to be easy. With sullen reluctance she shouldered her M16 and followed the APC as it backed into a narrow street beside the church.

Not bothering to listen as the major put the position to those inside, Thorne calculated the quantity of explosive he would need to blast a way in. "A couple of pounds of plastic will open the door. Save your lungs, Major, let me have my turn."

"Do that and we might just catch one of them behind it. Let's see if Sergeant Hyde can find another entrance first. A side door ought to be easier to force than these great things." Damn it, damn them! Revell was tempted to give loud vent to his feelings for the benefit of the civilians, but knew it wouldn't help, might even have the detrimental effect of reinforcing their obduracy if at the moment they were wavering. Telling them what he thought of them might be good for him, but it would as certainly eliminate any last chance of their cooperating.

Using the butt of the assault shotgun he hammered on the deep grained wood and called one last time. Still there was no response. The timber of the door seemed to absorb all his words, but he felt sure they must have heard him. Damn them!

"There's a side door, but . . ." Hyde had immediately to crush the rising hopes his first words had brought, ". . . but it's made like this one, on a smaller scale, and I can hear them stacking pews or something against it."

With the sergeant's report removing any lingering hope that they might effect a non-violent entry, still Revell grasped at one last straw. "Thorne, you're the engineer, before we resort to brute force of the explosive kind, any other suggestions as to how we might get inside?"

"The only thing I can think of, Major, is to try nudging the doors with the APC. Using crawler gear they'd have to give eventually, the brute weighs the best part of thirty tons. Those steps wouldn't be any problem but this would." Thorne slid his boot on the smooth worn stone of the porch. "No grip. The track'd just scrabble round and round."

"All right, the plastic it is, but the bare minimum. I want to take those civies back alive, not in an assortment of body bags."

"It'll just be an angel's tap, Major." Having worked the lump of gray material until it was pliable, Thorne began to tamp it into an inch wide where the halves of the door came imperfectly together. "Of course, if I had my way I'd wouldn't piddle about like this, I'd use a satchel charge and blow it, them and the whole bloody place off the face of the map. But, like the true artist I am, I know when restraint and understatement are called for, so for you I put aside the trowel and take up the palette knife."

190

"Have you finished?"

"Ready when you are, Major. Just putting the fuse in now. Eh, while this isn't on the scale I usually do things, I still think it might be sensible to, eh, take cover."

Thorne turned around to find he was talking to himself.

CHAPTER FOURTEEN

The antiseptic cream he'd dabbed on, and the bandage he'd wrapped about his hand had done nothing to ease Gross's pain. Blood continued to seep through the soiled white windings.

Out of sight at the far end of the church Webb could be heard dragging heavy carved furniture to pile against the side entrance. Edwards was laid on the bare stone by the font close to the main doors, where they'd dumped him when they had to clear the back of the Rangerover to find the tools for the wheel change.

He looked about for Sherry Kane. She'd gone into a little side chapel, and he noticed how she swayed unsteadily on her feet. Nearly falling she had to clutch at a small altar for support and then slumped to the red carpet before it.

"Not feeling too good?" Gross stood over her, playing with his erection through his trouser pocket. "Fancy a bit of this to buck you up?" Fuck it, he was running out of time. There would never be another opportunity and he'd always wanted to do it to her, ever since he'd seen her in that first film, when all those blokes had tossed off into her face. He'd have given anything to have changed places with each of them in turn, and have her blow bubbles and gurgle his with his spunk.

They were still shouting outside, but he paid no attention. Slowly, enjoying the anticipation, he unzipped himself and eased the rigid lump of flesh into the open. The air felt cool on it, and holding it at its broad base by two fingers he wagged it over her head.

"Look at this. Any of the studs in your films ever have one this size?"

"Get away from me, you pervert." Sherry would have screamed for help, but she hadn't the strength. It felt like she was burning up, and her energy was leaking away with the sweat that soaked and trickled down inside her clothes. Even holding up her head took an effort she could barely sustain and then her supporting arms gave way and she dropped to sprawl full length on her back.

"That's more like it. Here, let me do that." Brushing aside the weak movements of her limp hands over the tight crotch of her jeans he fumbled at her zip, seeing encouragement in the gesture, not the rejection that was intended.

The denim gaped to reveal pale blue cotton briefs, and as Gross tugged at her tightly cinched belt and unfastening it began to haul her jeans off, he felt the heat rising from her body.

194

"You're ready for me then, good and hot. I like a nice warm cunt." A band of acute discomfort, almost pain, tightened across his large stomach and caused him to pause, but it passed, and having managed to get her jeans to her knees his hands went greedily to the waistband of her underclothes.

"Not a real blonde then? Nice bush, what's it hiding?" Even as the scrap of damp material slid over her thighs he let his thumbs rake through her pubic hair, tracing the deepening groove within them. This time he tried to ignore the severe muscular twinge in his stomach, but wasn't entirely successful and had once more to wait for it to pass before he could jam his fingers between her legs and force them as far apart as the constricting garments around her knees would allow.

Sherry could make no effective effort to prevent him from getting into a press-up position over her, and slowly lowering his corpulent body toward contact with hers.

"You ready? Good and juicy? Looks like you're working up a good lather." He'd have liked to have dangled his balls on her, dragged them over her heat radiating belly, but his big erection had caused them to contract into a compact pouch beneath him as the skin was stretched tight.

"I'll have a quick one first, just to get rid of some of the load. Don't worry, they'll be plenty left if you fancy giving it a suck afterwards . . ."

Sensing the beginning of the return of the gut ache he steeled himself for it, but this time the savage cramping struck with tenfold intensity. It didn't help, only made it worse. Starting in his stomach the spasm wrenched down through his intestines.

"Oh no, not fucking now . . ." Gross hurled himself off the woman even as he was about to thrust forward into her body. Hampered by his loosened clothing, gathering it together about himself, he managed just a couple of steps before his bowels opened noisily.

Foul smelling liquid ran down his legs. He couldn't control it, and with each spasm came another gush of the watery excreta. Doubling with agony, frightened and weakened by the violent diarrhea, he collapsed.

At the same instant the whole building reverberated to a sharp explosion and a cloud of smoke blew in from the doorway and rose among the exposed beams of the roof, lit in shifting bands by the light filtering through the high set windows.

"It hasn't bloody worked." First to reach the still closed doors, Burke leaned against them, and was precipitated inside as they swung open at the light touch.

"Phew. Someone has dropped his guts." Pegging his nose with thumb and forefinger, Dooley sidled in and from behind a carved draught screen and looked about the interior.

"Search the place . . ." Taking a step into the smoke-blued gloom, past Burke who was picking himself up, it was Revell who found the first of the

196

civilians, his foot coming down on Professor Edwards's ankle. ". . . there're others."

Cautiously they fanned out to advance along all three aisles simultaneously. It was Hyde who discovered Gross and the woman.

"Phew, you sure are lucky you can't smell that fat guy, Sarge." Ripper had abandoned the spartan comfort of the Marder's bench seat and tagged along behind the searchers. Finding he hadn't back-tracked far enough, he took several more steps to get clear of the worst of the stench. "Times like this I wish I'd had my nose burned off."

Hyde turned his graft-patched face to the American, but said nothing. "Looks like these two were trying to make love, not war. All right, I'll take the man." He gripped Gross by the collar and started to tow him back to the door, leaving an intermittent slimy trail on the stone floor. "You bring the woman."

"Hey Sarge, I can't do that, I ain't fit for duty." Ripper illustrated his argument by flexing his shoulder, ceasing abruptly when he realized he wasn't creating the impression he'd wanted to.

Her temperature still soaring, Sherry Kane was unable even to react to the terrible sight of the sergeant's ghastly appearance. The fever that racked and shook her deprived her even of the strength to exhibit fear. She tried to talk to the other soldier, the young American, but couldn't. On his face was a curious expression as he stared at her half naked body, it was something she'd not seen any friend or client of hers display in a long time, it was embarrassment.

"Here, Dooley, can you give me a hand, I got to move her."

"So move her."

"I can't, not like this. It just ain't decent."

"Then pull her fucking knickers up." Like the others, Dooley had taken a good look at her, but he'd noticed her fever brightened dark rimmed eyes and perspiration smeared make-up as much as her semi-nakedness. "All that gabbing you do about the goings-on in those backwoods of yours, I wouldn't have thought this would have bothered you, or are you going to tell me you only know how to pull them down." He kept his thick gloves on and it made the task of making her decent that much more difficult. The tight fit of the fabric to her body didn't help and he had to keep turning her in order to inch the jeans over her wide thighs a fraction at a time.

"Shit, it weren't 'til I were going on for eighteen, when I met some city girls, that I even knew there were such things as underclothes. Back home I shoved my fingers and my tool up a load of skirts, but the only thing I'd ever found in my way was an occasional hand. It's just that it don't seem right touching her 'til we been introduced. Anyhow, I can see you ain't no gentlemen, keeping your gloves on."

"You show me a book of etiquette where it says I should take them off to do this and I'll think about it, until then I'm keeping them on."

"Very sensible." Burke had found an excuse to

come and oversee the operation. "I can feel the heat coming off her from here. Gloves might not stop you catching something, but every little precaution helps. You know, cleaned up, with some of that muck off her face and with about twenty pounds shed off her arse and hips, she'd be quite nice, not special but nice."

Sherry heard, and the tears that ran down her streaked face mingled with beads of perspiration and went unnoticed.

The sweep down the center aisle was led by Clarence, and as he came level with the lectern, he heard a noise from a dark corner beyond the choir stalls. Motioning the others to hold back he crept silently forward until he could see all but a small angle of the space.

High overhead there was a ragged bordered hole in the church roof. Bulks of timber and fragments of slate littered the floor below it and for some distance around. Taking another step it was impossible to avoid the shattered pieces and they grated beneath the sniper's boot.

It was not just the appalling smell of excreta that made him want to be out of there. Every breath he took brought also the oppressive scent of decay that pervaded the whole place, filling it and him to overflowing. "Come out. I haven't the patience to wait long."

There was no response, but Clarence heard the noise again, like that of an animal shuffling to compress itself into the smallest possible space.

Without looking he double checked that a round was chambered in the Enfield, and took the pace that would bring the whole of the poorly lit area into his field of vision. As he did a shaft of light streamed through the gaping roof and illuminated it graphically.

Stubble darkened Webb's chin and dust and cobwebs smothered the rest of his person. Concealment no longer possible, he stood and adopting a manner of haughty contempt, brushed himself. "I suppose it is your intention to kill me." He could not suppress the catch in his voice that betrayed his true emotional state. Fear showed also in his trembling hands, and he stuck them deep into his pockets to hide them.

"A tempting idea, better not mention it too often, there's others in the squad who might be unable to resist it."

Revell came forward, and noticed close by the remains of a human skeleton. A print dress that lay in moldy folds over the bones and a nearby bucket and mop marked it as that of a cleaner. The skull had been virtually destroyed by a smashing blow, and the weapon lay nearby.

The big metallic cylinder had burst apart on striking the unyielding surface of the floor. Revell pointed it out to the civilian. "Have you seen what you've been sharing your hidey-hole with?"

"Of course. Another of your filthy American chemical weapons. You can't frighten me with it, it has been there a long time, the contents will be inert by now."

"When you commie lovers get it wrong, you certainly do it in the biggest possible way." Taking up the mop, Revell ran it along the side of the crushed cylinder. "We must have some pretty smart armorers, seeing as how they'd have to load munitions where all the handling instructions are stencilled on in Russian."

"A trick, to put the blame elsewhere."

"Well if a fairy story like that gives you peace of mind, then you think that. I suppose there's no way I can make you believe that's not a US chemical weapon?"

"That's correct, none at all." Webb succeeded in injecting sneering condescension into his words, but even to him it was not entirely convincing.

"Pity. I thought I might have been doing you a favor by telling you I've seen one of those before, not as big though. It's a free fall munition the Russians developed for the Vietnamese to use in Cambodia, and used themselves in Afghanistan. They're supposed to make a retarded fall and scatter their contents at a predetermined altitude as they come down. Looks like the 'chute failed on this one and the dispersal mechanism was activated."

"So? Of what interest can this be to me." There was a tight dryness in Webb's throat, and something of his affected composure was evaporating.

"Like I said, it's not a chemical weapon. It's actually designed to deliver lots and lots of nasty little beasties called bacteria. From them you can get any one of a hundred very unpleasant diseases, most of which you haven't even heard of, and certainly wouldn't like to contract. We call them plague bombs."

"I demand that you treat me . . . for . . . for whatever I may have caught . . . immediately."

"Of course we will, soon as we get back. Have to wait and see what you develop before we can start pumping anything into you."

There was no way that Revell was going to tell the terrified man that in all probability either dehydration or ultra-violet light from the sun had rendered the biological agent harmless, and that the cleaner had been its first and last victim. He couldn't touch the civilian, but he could terrify him and let him inflict the torment of abject fear upon himself at least for a while.

Revell was a realist. He knew there would be no jail sentence for Webb or such of the others as should survive, when they finally got back to England or the States. Most likely Webb would be allowed to go quietly into early retirement, kept in comfort by an inflation proofed state pension. None of this would ever surface in the press. The many agents of influence the communists still had deeply implanted in the British civil service would see to that. Neat cover stories would be furnished to explain away the death of the others, under the guiding hand of KGB controllers the whole affair would be smoothed over and hidden away forever.

As a pale faced Webb was herded toward the entrance, Revell was tempted into serious consideration of Andrea's solution to any unsatisfactory situation. For her life was much more simple. She saw everything as either good or bad, and what she thought of as bad she swept away in a hail of automatic fire. But he had his orders, and knew that the extent of the retribution he could inflict on the traitor was to let him hold for as long as possible the mistaken belief that he had been contaminated.

"We can't take these three with us." Thorne surveyed the line of sick in the porch. "They're all stretcher cases, we haven't got the room."

"I wouldn't fancy having them as company even if they were fit, with all of them screaming, scratching, sweating, puking and shitting I'm even less keen." Dooley moved upwind of Gross. The fat man's bowels were open all the time and a thin trickle of sluggish fluid ran along a time worn groove in the porch and down the stone steps.

"Put them in their own transport then . . ."

"Won't work, Major." Hyde had anticipated that. "I've checked, and they've not enough fuel for the return journey. The Marder uses diesel so we can't even siphon some into the Rangerover."

"They want to meet their friends the Russians," unable to stay away any longer, Andrea pushed through the men to stand threateningly over the prisoners, "let me see to it that they are still here when the communists arrive." She levelled her rifle at the civilians.

* * *

It would be close, uncomfortably close, but his men would get there first. Rozenkov could enjoy a degree of satisfaction at knowing how great Morkov's anger and frustration would be at having his men just beaten in the race to intercept the delegation.

The liaison officer had almost caught him. From the very start of the operation he'd been deliberately misinforming him by incorrectly positioning the pins marking the GRU units. It was not by much, not sufficient to be immediately detectable in the satellite pictures, but enough to make a difference in the last lap, if the trick hadn't been spotted.

Again he read Morkov's intercepted radio message. It was simple, brutal, uncompromising. The closest GRU company was ordered to contact the civilians before the KGB, or else. There was no time for games any more, the maneuvering, the intrigue, had ceased.

Only by being able to do both well had Rozenkov worked his way to his present position, but as important to him had been knowing when to replace the velvet glove with the spiked knuckle duster.

There was something he had almost forgotten to do. Picking up the phone, he was put through to the duty room. "Rozenkov . . . Advise the building's security staff that Major Morkov is to be arrested the moment he returns. Also, have a section keep watch on his apartment should he go there instead, the same action to be taken. Inform me immediately, oh yes, and there is no need for restraint. I would like the major to be made aware of my displeasure."

Strangely he could almost feel, not sympathy,

rather an understanding of the man. In a way Morkov was much as he had been twenty years before, but he'd learned a lesson the major would now never get the opportunity to, of knowing when to let a chance go, of balancing risk against reward.

In all probability Rozenkov could have got this far five years earlier, if he'd been prepared to gamble once or twice, but instead he'd chosen to take the slower but more certain safe way to the top. In fact, thinking back he could recall others who, accepting risks he'd declined had paid dearly for their impetuous ambition.

A check of his watch and a simple calculation told him that the helicopters would be making their rendezvous shortly. Sure as he was of success, he would still feel better when those civilians were safely aboard and on their way to a reception by the gathering representatives of the world's media. Reaching to turn on the radio, he felt he could already begin composing his announcement to the Central Committee . . .

It was the second-in-command of the unit who came on the air, and that immediately brought Rozenkov's full attention back to the operation. If all had been as it should be then his senior would have answered. In the communist system seconds-in-command were used to do the dirty work, break bad news, accept blame.

"Give me your position." The coldness in Rozenkov's tone reflected the sensation in the pit of his stomach, and then he knew it was justified, when the map references he received showed the gunships to be sixty kilometers short of where they should have been.

"Why has there been a delay?" Ice filled his belly. ". . . I do not want to hear about mechanical failures, I want to hear nothing but that you have made the interception and have the civilian delegation on board . . . I do not care . . . use your best speed regardless . . . If the other falls behind, if it falls apart in mid-air, I do not care. You must make that interception, keep this channel open, I shall be listening."

Fools, idiots. He would kill them with his bare hands and his teeth if they failed. There was nothing more he could have done to stress the importance of their mission, and they had reduced speed when a fault had developed aboard the second gunship. It was unbelievable, after everything, to have it all put at risk by an overcautious pilot worrying about vibration from a gearbox.

Of one thing he could be sure, both aircrews would now be piling on all the speed they could. Normally there would have been conversation between the two craft, but they knew he would catch every word and so communication was kept to a bare minimum, mostly the passing of information and advice about the faulty drive shaft.

Rozenkov listened dispassionately as first an increase in vibration, then a rise in the temperature of the transmission oil, and then a fire were reported. He heard the frantic efforts by the flight deck crew to get the automatic extinguishers to function, and their anguish and desperation when they failed and the flames began to spread. Their words came as a garbled stream of curses and invective and pleading. Though he didn't touch the volume control Rozenkov heard the shouting go louder and louder until suddenly it was gone.

It was a little while before he heard the call-sign of the remaining craft. The pilot's voice was a shade too high, his delivery a little too fast.

". . . report that KGB helicopter gunship seven-four-nine has exploded in mid-air at low altitude. There are no survivors. I . . . I await your further orders."

"There is no change. You are no longer handicapped by the other craft, that is good. Now you should make better time . . ."

CHAPTER FIFTEEN

Bullets ricocheted about the entrance to the church, smacking razor-like fragments from the stone with every impact.

Andrea's reaction was fastest, finger already on the trigger, she swivelled and fired a whole magazine from the hip, then followed it with a rifle grenade in the direction of the Russian scout car that had appeared at the end of the street.

"Back inside." More of the heavy machine gun rounds followed the first long burst as Revell grabbed the fat man by a wrist made slippery by the obnoxious pool it lay in and towed him back into the shelter of the building. "Clarence, find the entrance to the bell tower, see what we're up against. That little wagon wouldn't have had a go at us if it'd been on its own."

All of the squad were safe, though Thorne's face bled from cuts made by slicing stone chips, but in the confusion of the scramble to get into cover, Webb had seen his chance and made a break.

Revell saw the civilian run to the Rangerover and jump in to start it. He levelled his shotgun at the vehicle, but held his fire as it began to accelerate toward the armored four-wheeler, now joined by a second, turretless, version.

Having to duck while more of the tracer laced bursts drilled and smashed the fabric of the porch, when he looked again Revell saw that the Rover was stalled after a glancing collision with a derelict truck. He could hear the starter motor whirring fruitlessly, see Webb furiously wrenching the ignition key in and out time after time.

The center section of the peaked roof of the second armored car began to elevate, and beneath it as it rose could be seen the snouts of a row of anti-tank rockets. Flame spurted from the rear of that mounted on the far left and the missile shot from its launch rail.

Thrashing filaments of wire snaked behind it as it dipped and arced along the road. Webb had his head down, was trying to ram home the gearlever with both hands, and never saw it coming. At the instant before impact the missile rose and almost soared over its target, but the side of the warhead clipped the roof of the Rangerover and that grazing impact was enough.

There was hardly any smoke. The interior of the estate car filled with raging fire that blasted every window from the bodywork. An arm and a head topped by blazing hair were briefly visible before flame totally enveloped the vehicle with the explosion of its fuel tank.

Another missile leaped from the elevated launcher.

210

Throwing himself into the church to escape the concussion of its detonation against the steps, Revell ran into Clarence.

"It's going to get rougher, Major. There's only those two made it so far, but there's a troop of tanks struggling to get through that flood beyond the town and a couple of APCs trying to work their way around. They're making heavy going of it, but they'll be here inside of fifteen minutes or so."

Again the porch was blasted by the shock wave from a near miss, and both doors were ripped from their wrought iron hinges and toppled into the church, their landing adding to the dust already raised.

"Clear the side door, we'll get out that way."

"And what about them?" Hyde had pulled the three sick civilians well inside to make sure they escaped the attention of the lethal fragments and chunks of debris beginning to find their way further and further inside the building as the Russian vehicles closed in for the kill. "We're kidding ourselves if we think we can take them with us. The old guy has been near enough skinned alive by that mustard, the flesh is just peeling off him. That woman is running such a fever her heart could give out any moment and the fat bloke looks like he's got cholera just as bad as he could have. He'll never last, none of them will."

"Let me finish them." Pushing in front of the NCO, Andrea confronted the officer. "It is not possible to take them, mine is the only way."

"No, no. We'll leave them for the Russians to nurse and bury." Revell reached the side door as Boris and Thorne pulled the last of the barricade down. He

211

stooped to leave through the low doorway, then hesitated and ushered the others through first. "You too."

Andrea had hung behind, and was fitting a fresh magazine to her M16 when the major beckoned. "Do you think I would risk being left behind just so that I could kill those animals?"

"I know you would."

The alley was a dead end, and the buildings to either side were too substantial for the Marder to bulldoze its way to safety through them. Burke was left with only one alternative, a high speed run up the main street, offering the Russian gunners a clear shot at their light rear armor. "Hang on, you lot."

"Be ready for a fast bail-out if we take a hit." Checking the hatch above his head, Revell tried the quick release catch and was relieved to find it worked smoothly.

"Fucking marvelous, ain't it." Like the others Dooley was divesting himself of as many encumbrances as possible, anything that might impede a hurried exit. "Here we are whose shitty paper-thin armor is hard put to keep out a heavy machine gun round, and now we're about to offer an easy up-the-arse shot to a commie tank destroyer."

"I've been watching it in action, its crew are not the world's best." That was the only consolation Revell could offer. "Let's go, and try to keep that fire and the wrecks between us and that tank-killer."

Burke took the engine revs as high as they would go before crashing the Marder into gear. The big machine leaped forward and carried away a corner of a building as it skidded through a canting turn into the main street.

Using the remotely controlled rear mounted machine gun Ripper poured tracer and armor piercing rounds at the unmoving armored cars, concentrating his fire on their vision ports and periscopes. "They ain't following!"

"They don't bloody have to." Firing from a side ball mounting Dooley let fly with an Uzi at a Russian infantryman aiming an anti-tank rocket from his shoulder.

Thrown back by the several impacts, the man sent the warhead on its way as he fell, but it flew wildly astray, taking the tiles from a distant shop roof.

More of the squad were engaging infantry targets, and a long jet of red flame shot from the turret to splash and lick around the sides of a rusting bus. A section of Russian soldiers staggered into view wreathed from head to foot in rippling flame.

"Those commie shits have left their battle taxis for once and come in on foot." Throwing the Marder in a lurching side swipe at a handcart, Burke succeeded in overturning it on the machine gun team using it as cover to pour a storm of bullets into the APC's front quarter.

"We're nearly through . . ."

Revell didn't know who it was who had tempted providence, and there wasn't time to find out, there was just long enough after Ripper shouted a warning to tense themselves for the impact and then an anti-tank rocket struck the personnel carrier's rear.

It was like being in a bucket being hammered by a

madman. The thunder of the detonation was followed instantly by the squealing of scraping metal as a track broke apart and gouged scoops of metal from the armor. Crabbing first to the left as several road wheels were blown off by the explosion, the Marder swerved hard right as large pieces of wreckage jammed the other track, then stopped.

"Flame all around, then every one out." Through the prisms in the command cupola Revell saw billowing gouts of fire pour death into every side alley and nearby window, then as the last burst fell short with the tanks exhausted, all the hatches were thrown open and they went out shooting. As he jumped, he tossed a thermite grenade back inside and heard it crackle into white hot life as they ran across the street.

A grenade from Andrea's launcher blew in the door of a house, another tossed through a window by Hyde made sure it was cleared and they raced inside, barging through its musty hall, hurdling a grinning corpse and stampeding out through the kitchen and across its once neat vegetable garden.

Boris and Dooley set up a rear guard as the others climbed iron railing around a school yard, and caught a Russian following them too closely. He went down like a felled tree with a bullet through his neck.

An attempt to establish a machine gun post at the upper window of an overlooking house fared no better. Andrea put her first grenade in neatly through it and the resulting explosion threw an arm onto a greenhouse roof.

Bones and skulls and scraps of clothing were scattered as they dashed through the sun-dried bodies on the playground. Clarence couldn't bring himself to

214

go that way, and skirting it, ran straight into a section of Russian infantry coming around the side of the school building.

There was a rage inside of him that begged to be let loose, and he unleashed it on the lieutenant who led them, putting a bullet into his stomach and then two more into the chests of the men to either side of him. At that range, with the tip of the Enfield's barrel almost touching them, the dum-dum bullets burst their targets apart and showered those following with blood and tissue.

The rest of the section turned and fled, and more shots followed them, each with neat precision tearing a chunk of vertebrae from the base of a spine or shattering the back of a cranium. Last of them to die was a slant eyed Mongol whose thick short neck was almost severed by a mushrooming soft cored round. His body toppled among those of the children and stained their faded clothes and bleached bones with vivid gouts of fresh blood.

"They're giving up, they ain't following." Every pace brought new pain to Ripper as the scar tissue forming over his burns was stretched and broken by the jarring strain of keeping up with the others.

Only a smattering of single shots chased them across the strip of plowed land behind the school, and even that petered out as they reached the steep slope of the valley wall.

"It is not that they are giving up," blood trickled from beneath the cuff of Boris's smock and over his hand to drip from his fingers, "it is that we no longer matter to them. They have what they want." There was only a dull sensation of discomfort from the

215

bullet wound in his forearm, and when he reached for a handful of pliant branches of a young pine to pull himself up a difficult section between craggy boulders, he was relieved to find he had the unimpaired use of the limb, there was no fracture. Until now he'd been frightened to use it, expecting agony and the confirmation of its being shattered when he did. Inside his sleeve there was a growing damp stickiness.

"I told you we should not leave them." Andrea didn't care that her words might carry to others besides the officer. "You should have let me finish them. The Russians will make much use of them, and you will have failed."

There was no one else Revell would have let speak to him like that, certainly no one else in the squad. He resented what she said, and for the first time realized that having her close was not always going to be fun. Her way of reducing all situations to black and white was not his. In the church he'd been presented with a far more complex decision than she realized. It was not a simple choice between eliminating a few worthless traitors or letting the Russians win. She offered him the option of permitting an atrocity, of being party to a war crime and that he couldn't do. Damn it, that was what they were fighting.

All of them at various times complained at how the NATO forces were forced to fight clean while the communists used every dirty trick in the book plus many more of their own invention, but when it came to it, when they had the choice of doing things that way themselves, inevitably they balked.

This wasn't the time or place he could explain all

that too her, that's if she'd even been prepared to try to understand, and so he said nothing, exaggerating the difficulty of the scree slope he was negotiating and pretending absorption with that to the exclusion of all else,

The ground rose fast, near vertical in places and within a short while they were looking down on the roofs of the village, spread in a ribbon along the floor of the valley. Twice they had to call a halt to enable Ripper and Boris to catch up, and both times took advantage of the respite to gulp air into their into their aching lungs.

"Either I'm getting old, or we're a good way above sea level." Dooley eased the straps of his pack and rifle as they started up again.

"Bit of both I expect, but mostly it must be the old dames you go with sucking the life as well as your spunk out of you." Burke looked at Dooley struggling to climb a difficult patch, a slope littered with shale-like stone that slid away from beneath his feet as he placed them. "Help a bit if you got rid of that pack. It could have cost you your bloody life if it'd snagged as we bailed out. Still could if it drags you off this fucking mountain."

"There ain't no way I'm chucking this." Dooley hitched its straps more securely onto his shoulders, sliding back some distance as he did. "This is my shitty future in here, where I go it goes."

"Shut your gabbing and climb." They were becoming spread out, and Revell recognized the danger of their becoming separated in this broken country. The journey back on foot was going to be hard and long, tackling it as individuals they would stand no chance, sticking together for mutual support they would.

A last effort and they made the crest, to find themselves on a knife edge ridge that fell away as steeply before them as the climb they'd just completed. Away into the distance stretched a succession of similar features, interspersed with hills that were little more than piles of rock dotted with sparse stands of fir and pine. They were as devoid of color as the bare hills, leached of life by the poisonous yellow rain the Russians used in such concentrations.

Before starting the descent, Revell looked back at the church. All he could see was the tower and a part of the roof, none of the activity that he knew there would be around it. Beyond the compact confines of the small settlement, still stranded amid the flood waters like beached whales were the Russian tanks. Tiny figures waded about them, working without sign of urgency.

As he was about to give the order to move, Revell caught a glint of bright reflected light further down the valley, and then heard the beat of the gunships' blades thrashing through the thin air. The sun flashed again from the domed canopies of the tandem cockpits, and as the chopper banked he saw the weapons operator hunch over his sights.

During his pacing of the room Rozenkov had approached the radio a dozen times, and the telephone as often. He'd touched neither. If ever he got his hands on Major Morkov . . . As far as Department A of the KGB was concerned the whole operation had become a disaster, and far worse than that for him personally. To think, only hours before such power had been not just within his reach but actually in his grasp, and now it was about to be torn from him.

At least he had some small consolation in knowing that Military Intelligence was not likely to come out of it well either. The last intercepted message had shown them calling urgently for medical assistance. There would be no impressive press conferences, no television interviews. All that the GRU had gained was a trio of dying civilians. If they had any sense they would not try to make overmuch of that, the capitalist editorials would soon point out which side it was that had seeded the area with toxins and bacteria . . .

It came to him suddenly, and he knew it was the only solution, the only way by which he could hope to salvage something. He grabbed the phone. "Connect me with the Kremlin. I wish to speak with Comrade Politburo member Ivan Forminski." The wait seemed interminable. "Then put me through to him at his dacha, it is of the highest priority." Again there was a long delay as Moscow's telephone system torturously routed the call through the several manual switchboards involved.

"Rozenkov, Colonel Rozenkov, Head of Department . . . Yes, I'll wait . . . Comrade Forminski? It is Rozenkov. Forgive my asking, Comrade, is this a secure line? . . . Then I shall try to be as clear as I can, Comrade Forminski. It is about the deal that was discussed recently at the meeting . . . yes Comrade, the one that is of special interest . . . Yes," he changed hands and wiped his sweaty palm on the side of his jacket, "I have to tell you that the foreign goods have become spoiled . . . I understand your disappointment, Comrade . . . The contamination is due to interference and clumsy handling by another member of our cooperative . . . Then would our customer rather wait for another consignment?"

The minute he waited for the reply was the longest of Rozenkov's life, dragging on forever. It came, a single word. "Thank you Com . . ." He was talking to himself. As he shakily replaced the receiver he had to sit, he was shattered, utterly drained.

He would not be getting that immediate confirmation of his appointment, it and the promotion would have to be gained the hard way by three months' grinding slog at petty detail. But at least he had that second chance, if he tidied the loose ends in a satisfactory manner, discreetly, thoroughly. And in doing just that he could extract a measure of revenge on Military Intelligence, whose meddling had almost cost him his career. He reached for the radio . . .

On that bare ridge, with no scrap of cover, they were a sitting target. Revell pulled Andrea into a shallow cleft in the rock and used his own body to block it.

As the gunship dipped closer he could see the heavy weapon load slung from its stub wings and the cluster of cannon barrels projecting from its chin turret.

The range closing, Revell sensed the moment had passed when the chopper would use its missiles or cannon, now his attention was on the tear-drop shaped cannisters nestling among the rocket pods. All he could hope was that the napalm hit them square on, then it would be fast. If the weapon operator's aim was a little off then instead of being engulfed by the heart of the fireball they would be spattered by fist sized blobs of the burning mixture that would adhere to them and transform them into writhing human torches.

Others of the squad were firing, emptying the magazines of their rifles and sub-machine guns toward the gunship. Andrea tried to push past Revell to use hers, but he kept her pinned inside the narrow crevice. Though many must have struck, the gunship's titanium armor shrugged aside the small caliber rounds.

Closing his eyes, Revell awaited the sheet of flame, but the wall of air that buffeted him was cool, carrying with it not the deluge of blazing petrol-jelly he'd anticipated, but sharp grit and stinging dust.

Banking away, the helicopter began a wide turn down into the valley. Relaxing his grip on the rock, Revell was pushed aside by the girl as she took hasty aim and sent a long burst after the gunship.

That fire was as ineffectual as the rest had been, and unharmed the chopper maintained its wide descending turn. At two hundred feet above the valley floor it levelled out and raced in over the village from the west.

Against the eye-confusing clutter of the rooftops Revell didn't see the drop tanks go, but the gash of red flame along the main street was clear enough, and its twin that engulfed the houses behind the church.

. . . two, three, four . . . To himself Revell counted

221

off the second then watched the expanding white fire envelop every inch of the center of the village, only the very tip of the bell tower showing above the intensely bright bubble of flame.

Many of the houses, their walls bursting under the intense pressure created by the searing blast, seemed to implode, falling in on themselves. Others, beyond the circle of devastation wrought by the super-na-palm, steamed and smoked and began to burn.

A huge ball of black smoke rose over the village, to reveal blow-torch like feathers of red and yellow roaring from the church's every door and window.

Only one of the bogged down T84s brought its anti-aircraft mount into action against the gunship as it flew over, and then only in hesitant bursts that signalled the gunner's confusion as to what was happening.

"Looks like you got what you wanted after all. The Russians have done it for you." As the sound of the helicopter's engines faded into the distance, Revell held out his hand to assist Andrea over the last few feet to the crest of the ridge.

He hadn't expected her to, but she took it, and her fingers enmeshed with his as she hauled herself up. For a moment he forgot what he was going to say. "Right . . . So let's put in some distance. There's a long way to go."

That was an understatement, but Revell could have made light of anything. As they started down he was aware that Andrea was close by him, even when the going became so treacherous that the descent called for all his attention.

This was what he'd wanted. It had been a long time

coming, but she was with him now, and he'd keep it that way. To hell with the past, to hell with Inga, with the bitch, with everything.

So long as Andrea was with him in the Zone he was going to enjoy making war, and together they'd be making plenty of it.

GREAT BOOKS

E-BOOKS

AUDIOBOOKS

& MORE

Visit us today

www.speakingvolumes.us